THE QUEEN OF THIEVES

ANNIE SHIELDS

PART I

CHAPTER 1

London, 1879

Trixie

"What are we supposed to do, Angela? How will we live?"

For a fleeting moment, Trixie watched the unyielding veneer under the overly rouged cheeks slip on her sister's face as she looked across the room to her. She saw as her gaze danced between her two younger siblings that stood before her, clinging to each other. And for that moment, Trixie felt hope curl in her belly. But then, the mask was back on, and Angela carried on bundling her clothing into a burlap sack.

"It's not my problem," Angela spat. "You weren't meant

to be here. You're eight – you're old enough to get work. You were supposed to be out trying to earn some coin,"

Trixie had known deep in her gut that something was wrong with her big sister. She had sensed it when Angela had left without a word earlier that morning. She'd wondered if maybe something was worrying her – after all, with two mouths to feed, it was a lot for Angela to be responsible for. Maybe that was why she had steered her youngest sibling Lily back towards the slum early that day.

"I tried," Trixie said, her tears stinging the backs of her eyes from Angela's scornful tone. "No one had any work for two kids like us,"

"You said we were a family!" Lily cried out, less in control of her emotions than Trixie was. "You swore you wouldn't leave as Pa did! You promised!"

Angela pulled the bag off the rickety table and let loose a sigh. "You can stay until the end of the week. The rent is paid until then, but you shouldn't…" A voice from the street below shouted her name followed by a string of curses and Angela's lips thinned. She looked down at her two younger siblings, clinging to each other. "I have to go. And so must you. You cannot stay here, okay? Sooner or later, you will end up on your own. May as well be now,"

"Don't leave us!" Lily shouted and lunged for Angela, trying to hold onto her but Angela flicked off the little girl as if she were an annoying animal. Trixie pulled her back, holding a sobbing Lily close to her chest. She listened to Angela's receding steps as she clomped down through the tenement building. She longed to go to the window, to look down into the street and see who it was who had lured her sister away, but it would be futile trying to look down through the thick grime that coated the glass. Instead, she lowered them to the floor and waited for Lily to settle.

"It'll be fine, you'll see," she stroked Lily's brown hair, so similar in colouring to her own, and pressed a kiss to it as their mother used to do to hers.

"Everybody leaves me," Lily hiccupped, knuckling away the tears.

"Not me," Trixie smiled at her, "I won't leave you, ever."

Lily lowered her gaze and lifted a shoulder. "Pa did. Angela did. Ma and Sophie did," she added quietly.

"Mama and Sophie are in Heaven with the other angels," Trixie said solemnly. Memories of the day when their life had changed flickered through her mind, though she would never share the horrors with Lily. The little girl had only ever known a life of living here, too young to remember the time before their father had taken to drinking his wage away or remember when they had had windows they could see through and had a front door of their own. "Mama was kind and good, and I know that she wouldn't have wanted to leave you."

"Why did Papa leave?" Lily lifted her tear-stained face to her sister.

Trixie longed to be able to answer her but didn't really know. She only knew that he'd simply stopped coming home, and Angela had had to find a way to earn money to pay the rent. She'd brought them here and that had been their life since.

"It's gone cold," Trixie pushed to her feet, dislodging Lily from her lap, and avoiding her question. "Shall we light the fire?" She opened the tinder box next to the stove and angled it towards the low light filtering through the glass. Black coal dust in the bottom slid to the corner and Trixie bit back the sigh. "Never mind. We'll just sleep under the blanket, okay? I'll keep you warm."

She held up the ratty blanket that was pooled on top of the coir mattress in the corner and lay down next to Lily, covering them both up. She hummed a soft tune and stroked her hair. In the fading daylight, as her little sister slowly settled to sleep, Trixie looked about the small room that had been home for the past two years. Crumbling walls and windows that the wind whistled through, a bare wooden floor that was uneven with a hole in the corner that was part of a rat run. She knew that they were luckier than most people. They had a table and two chairs, and the stove doubled up as a heater when they could afford a piece of coal. The house contained lots of rooms, all domains for families, stacked atop each other across several floors. Even now, Trixie could hear her neighbours, living their lives as if pressing on them through the wall.

At least it's not the workhouse.

Angela would say this often. Whilst she would send out her younger siblings to the market to sell flowers or find work on the stalls, she would be out for long hours and fetch home pig's trotters and eels, steaming chestnuts, or fresh bread slices that were sometimes still warm. Her stomach growled and she shoved away the thought of food. Instead, she needed to think of a way for the two of them to live. Trixie was the careful one, the conscientious one, her mother had once said. She had no idea how Angela had made her money, how she had kept a roof over their heads since she had brought them here. Now, she wondered if Angela had done it deliberately. And if she had, why?

Sounds of the tenement raged under her and sleep eluded her as she tried to think of a way to keep them both out of the workhouse.

≈

"MAYBE THE RENT collector forgot about us?"

Trixie eyed her sister's hopeful expression and had to stop herself from snorting. "A rent collector doesn't forget. You heard what they said downstairs. Every Monday, without fail, the rent is collected."

"But two Mondays have passed?"

Trixie nodded, leaning her head back against the wall that they were sat next to, her eyes drifting back towards the window. They'd been living in a state of fear, waiting on the dreaded collector to turn up, yet no one had. "The end of the week, Angela had said. I don't know what's happened, or why the rent collector hasn't knocked at our door. I only know that if we had had to pay, we wouldn't have afforded to eat. If we can find some regular work, we'll be okay, Lily." She sighed, exhaustion tugging at her. She was tired of worrying, of not knowing. She placed a hand against her stomach. "It feels like something is gnawing at my belly, I'm that hungry,"

"We tried everywhere though?"

"And we must keep trying, too. And pray that–" She paused to listen. Voices, loud and insistent, rumbled somewhere from deep inside the house. Urgent and... angry. Trepidation rippled through her. Instinctively, she wanted to hide. Looking about the room, there was nowhere big enough to secrete them both. Lily swung wide eyes to her sister as she listened. The sounds grew louder... closer. Trixie reached for Lily as footsteps marched up the wooden stairs and the two sisters clung to each other, staring at the thin door. Waiting.

When the door swung open, it wasn't a man who filled the doorway. She was beautiful and glamourous. Deep red hair was piled on top of her head, and the emerald-green dress that she wore was fitted to her voluptuous figure. She had flawless creamy skin; a vivid yellow stone winked at the base of her throat. Sharp eyes swept the room, alighting on the two small children who cowered in the corner. The gaze swept the room, her nose pinched white, thin lips peeled back in a smile as she stepped across the threshold and looked down at the children. Two wiry men flanked her in the doorway.

Lily tucked her face into Trixie's neck, whimpering.

Trixie lifted her chin, defiance radiating from her as she stared back at the woman.

The woman tilted her head as she considered the glare. The thin lips quirked up on one side. "Hello. I'm looking for Angel... though you might know her as Angela. And don't try and deny knowing her. You look too much like her not to be related,"

Trixie had to swallow on a dry throat before she was able to speak. "She left. Two weeks ago,"

The woman's dark eyes moved over the room more leisurely this time as she stepped further into the room, tugging on the fingers of her silk gloves. "That right? Did she say where she was going?"

Trixie shook her head. "She just went,"

"With a man!" Lily supplied, though her voice was muffled against Trixie's shoulder.

"Are you here for the rent?" Trixie asked, her voice hesitant.

The woman gave a husky laugh. "You could say that. I own this building. Do you have any money for me?"

Trixie shook her head, eyes narrowed. "Who are you?"

"Angel didn't mention me? I'm Stella. Your sister works for... worked for me," she held out her hand to one of the men, her eyes not moving from the two children. He reached into his pocket and removed a cigarette, then lit it and handed it to her. She inhaled from the tip, held the smoke before blowing it towards the ceiling. "How long have you lived here?"

"Since my Pa left. Angela found us this place,"

The woman sucked again, blew out another stream. "Your sister neglected to mention that she had siblings. She said the place was for her sick father. Come to think about it, no one ever had to call here for the rent as she always met the terms of our arrangement. Turns out that she was a better liar than a thief," the husky laugh came again, though Trixie didn't understand the joke. She pointed her cigarette at Trixie, dark eyes contracted against the smoke. The gemstones in her rings winked at them. "Are you hungry?"

Lily's head came round, though her head remained against Trixie. Neither child replied.

The woman sighed. "How old are you both?"

Trixie remained mute, though it was the ever-helpful Lily who mumbled, "I'm six, Trixie is eight."

"Trixie? That's a pretty name."

"It's Beatrix," Lily replied, her head coming up as she smiled at the woman. "I'm Lily,"

The woman took another inhale. "Are you hungry, Lily?" When she nodded her reply, the woman snapped her fingers and dispatched the men to go and find a street seller with food. "We can fix that for you. Would you like to come with me? Get you a nice bed and some proper food in your belly? Maybe a pretty dress?"

"We're fine here," Trixie put a protective forearm across her sister, "thank you for the offer. If you can give us a day or two, we'll find you some money for the rent."

The woman fixed her with a hard stare. "Oh, no. I won't trust a word that any of you White girls say ever again. You'll go where I say and do as you're told."

"But we don't have any rent for you?"

The man returned and the scent of roasted meat drifted through the room. Trixie's belly let out a growl as she eyed the greasy-looking paper bag.

"Oh, don't worry," Stella waved a hand at the man, indicating that he shares the food. "You both will be payment enough."

CHAPTER 2

$\mathcal{F}$elix

FELIX BAKER COUNTED the strikes of the village clock, much as he had since his father had taught him to count. From the farmhouse on the other side of the village where he'd spent his first ten years, the sound had been muted. But tonight, from within the vicarage, the gongs resonated much louder. He could see the crescent of the moon through the gap in the curtains and knew that the small village would be bathed in an eerie light. The air would be sharp and clear. Tomorrow, he should be helping his father with the farm, working the land, and tending to the animals. It had been that way for as long as he could remember. Instead, he lay in a strange bed, unsure where he would fit into this new house. Uncertain of what his future held.

When the door creaked open and the light from the oil lamp spilled across the polished wooden floor, Felix turned his head. The reverend's glasses reflected the light, and the old man's lips lifted slightly.

"Can't sleep?"

Felix shook his head. "No. The church bells are so loud,"

Frank Huxley nodded. "It took a while for me to get used to them when I first moved here. Now, I don't hear them. Do you know what might help? I could warm you up a cup of milk?"

Felix slid out of the bed covers, put on the dressing gown that was held out for him, and he followed the vicar through the quaint cottage, into the kitchen. "Mrs. Akerman always leaves me a snack for the night, in case I can't sleep." The vicar lit the light sconces around the room, and the light pushed back on the darkness. He set a pan onto the stovetop, stoked the coals as Felix clambered up onto the chair. He pushed a plate of biscuits towards Felix, who looked up at him, not wanting to appear rude. The vicar gestured to him. "Don't be shy. Her biscuits are the best I've ever tasted."

The housekeeper certainly had a reputation locally for her baking. Felix bit into the buttery crust and smiled around the mouthful. "S'good,"

"I know," Frank grinned at him, adding the warmed milk to two mugs. He set one in front of Felix, added a glug of whisky to his, and then he sat down across from the young boy. He blew at the steam, took a sip, put the cup down. "So…. What are we to do with you, Felix Baker?"

Felix's chewing slowed and he swallowed down on the suddenly dry crumbs in his mouth. "Mrs. Akerman said I should be grateful to you, and not give you any trouble. That if it wasn't for you, I'd be done for. Or in the workhouse, at least."

Frank sipped at his drink. "I'm not sure you'd be done for, Felix. But your father was a good man. A kind and generous Christian man. And the Lord teaches us to be kind and considerate to one another. To help others when they need it, and then there will be no more need. I wish that I could help all of God's children, but alas, I can't. But if I can only help one person, then that is better than helping no one. I believe that the Lord sent you to me to look after you, to teach me what it is like to be the father I have always wanted to be."

"You don't have your own children?"

"Not of my own, though I see everyone in my flock as part of my family," Frank took another drink, proffered the plate to Felix to take another biscuit. "So, we need to work out how to live together. I know that you like to be outside, working the land. Your father always spoke so highly of you. He was proud of you, Felix. Know that much,"

Felix blinked against the burning of his eyes, snapping small chunks off the cookie as he fought for control. "Why did the Lord take him away from me?"

Frank tapped the back of his hand. "Sometimes, it's just our time to go. But he sent you to me. We don't know what His plans are – and our human minds aren't strong enough to know why. That's why I read, to try and learn as much as I can about life before I'm called to heaven. Do you read?"

"Pa showed me some words. I didn't go to school. There was always too much to do on the farm."

"Would you like to go to school? Read about the Greats? History?"

Felix squashed one of the chunks, rubbed his fingers together so that he showered the bits on the table. "I think so. I like to know stuff."

Frank lifted the cup to his lips. "Then you should know that Mrs. Akerman doesn't like crumbs. Get a cloth and wipe those up. Then we'll go to the library and choose some books."

"Now? Shouldn't I be asleep?"

Frank chuckled. "Yes, you should. Do you want to go to bed or go on an adventure through the sands of time?"

Felix smiled, the first one since he'd watched his father's coffin go into the ground. "The time thing."

$\sim$

Why didn't I say no?

Trixie stared out of the carriage window and wondered what else she could have said to this strange woman who seemed used to barking out orders and getting her way without question. Lily was tucked up against Trixie, her thumb plugged into her mouth as she too tracked the busy London streets that they raced through.

Stella was lounging against the opposite door, her eyes half shut as the tang of smoke from her cigarette filled the interior of the cab. "Your sister better have run far," Only her lips moved with the muttered words. "No one leaves me. No one."

Trixie ignored her even as fear made sweat trickle down her sides. Questions raced through her mind though she refused to voice them to this formidable woman.

"Have you been in a carriage before?"

Trixie lifted her chin and the woman chuckled.

"Oh, girl, don't you try me. Better people have tried, and they have all failed. Look, you can cooperate with me, and I can give you a pleasant life. Or I can weight your ankles and drop you in the river. Those are your choices."

"You're the reason my sister left us," Trixie said dully.

Stella's hand shot across the space between them with lightning speed, gripping the thin wrist as her features twisted grotesquely. "Your sister left because she backed the wrong horse! Her mistake."

Shouts went up outside the carriage and clunking sounded as they jerked to a stop. The door opened and the box was set down. One of Stella's thugs stepped back, his eyes forward and his expression blank. Finally, Trixie met the stern look of Stella and tried to keep the panic out of her eyes.

"Choose wisely, Beatrix." Stella held her hand out and the thug assisted her down. She walked across the pavement and disappeared in through a heavy-looking oak door. The thug exchanged a few words with the other man who'd been in the house, and then he was alone on the streets with the two girls. His eye ran over the exterior of the building before he leaned in. Lily shrank back from him, and Trixie eyed him warily. He smiled a warm kind smile.

"It's not all bad," he said. "Angel... she wouldn't have left you unless she had to."

"You knew my sister?"

The smile deepened. "Everyone here knew her. I was where you are twenty years ago. Me Ma died and I was starving, running about with the rats. It wasn't fun, don't mind tellin' you. In there," he indicated the building with his head, "you'll at least get a hot meal and a roof over your head."

Trixie's eyes looked up at the building, the menacing stone exterior marred with soot and smoke. Bars covered the windows, like sad eyes that were staring out towards the docks. Gulls protested overhead, winging their way on the salty air. Similar squat buildings surrounded them, and smoke billowed from the factories that clustered around the warehouse.

"Will she really put us in the river?" Lily lisped at him.

The man sighed. "I've seen what she is willing to do to get what she wants. You want my advice? Take the offer, girls. It's not much of a choice but it'll be better than the workhouse…trust me."

Trixie met his eyes, her lower lip disappearing between her teeth. He was right – what choice had they been left with? Angela had been scared of this woman but, if she stayed, she might be able to find out why she left from the people who seemed to know more about her big sister than she did.

"Where do you sleep?"

His mouth quirked up on one side. "You ask a lot of questions, kid. Hurry up now, I have work to do. Come on!" Without waiting for permission, he slid his hands under Trixie's arms and swung her down, and had to catch Lily as she scrambled, terrified of being parted from her sister. "In you go and be quick about it!"

Trixie reached for her sister's hand, and she took a step before turning back. "What's your name?"

He used a thumb to push back the edge of his billycap. "George. No more questions – be off with you."

The door rattled and clunked before it swung wide and two girls in the black and white dress of maid's slipped out. Frowning as the two hurried off along the street away from her, Trixie turned back to George to ask who they were and why an industrial business needed maids, but he was pulling himself up into the carriage. She tracked the girls until they rounded the corner and as George hurried off, the pair were alone on the street. Beyond the door was dark, a looming cavern, and, swallowing down on the sense of doom, Trixie walked towards it and stepped through into the unknown.

CHAPTER 3

$\mathscr{T}$rixie

"WE DON'T WANT no street rats in 'ere!" A girl, not much older than Trixie, stepped around Stella and she walked towards them with a shooing motion. "Out!"

Stella's laugh sounded like rocks in a bucket as she turned her head. Triumph gleamed in her eyes when Trixie met a knowing look. "These are our new recruits, Maisie. It turns out Angel was keeping secrets from me – and these are her replacements."

Disapproval crossed the young girl's face. "They're filthy."

Stella harumphed. "Nothing that a bit of soap won't sort out. See that they're washed and dressed, and then bring them to me," She stalked off, her boots clinking off the wrought iron staircase in the corner that curled up to a mezzanine floor. Trixie could see the reflection of the glass from the windows up there.

Trixie looked about her. Someone had tried to make the space more homelike, with sparse items of dark wooden furniture and the occasional rug dotted around the grey slabbed floor. Wide, arching doorways opened off the space that they were stood in, the beams exposed overhead. Trixie spotted the pigeons that she could hear nesting above.

"No time to dillydally, girl," Maisie pushed Trixie in the back, meeting the scowl that was sent back at her head-on. "Stella doesn't like to be kept waitin', so get moving.'"

"Which way?"

Maisie lifted a finger and jabbed at the doorway to their right. "Don't be mouthing back at me. Just because you knew Angel, don't mean you'll get any favours from me."

Trixie took Lily by the hand and pushed the door open. Before her lay another vast area, though this one was crammed full of beds, lined up and all neatly made with white sheets and a navy blanket tucked under the mattress. Several pairs of eyes swung round to stare at the newcomers, and Trixie ducked her head, pulling Lily close to her side. The girls looked neat, and their dark dresses were clean. Two of them had rags around their heads to keep their hair back off their faces and held a mop in their hands.

"What you all starin' at? I know you have chores to do! You heard Stella this morning – I'm in charge until Lizzie gets out of Brixton clink and I won't have standards slippin'. Pick up that bucket!" Murmurs rippled throughout the group, but they were all spurred into action. "Follow me," She didn't wait to see if Trixie and Lily were following but wove her way around the bedsteads towards another offshoot of the room.

Trixie knew that the word 'clink' meant prison. *Was that why Angela had run? Just how much trouble had she been in?* She longed to ask for an explanation but instead, tugged on Lily's hand, not really wanting to inspire the wrath of Maisie any further, and she followed the other girl through the door, into a space that had several iron bathtubs in, along with buckets. A shelf run the length of one wall and was lined with countless bottles and boxes, filled with cleaning products judging by the floral smells that filled the air.

"Have you got lice? Probably," Maisie answered the question under her breath as she bent for a bucket. "Those rags won't be even worth tryin' to save," She eyed the grubby dresses that both girls stood in. "Get a bucket and follow me."

Several trips later, one of the baths was half-filled with tepid water, and the hem of Trixie's dress dripped a staccato beat on the floor around her bare feet.

"Right, take off your dress and get in,"

Trixie frowned and exchanged a confused look with her sister.

"What yer waitin' for? I ain't got all day, have I?"

"Why are we to bathe? These are the only clothes we own – what are you going to do with them?"

Maisie folded her arms and glared at Trixie. "You're bathing 'cause you're stinkin' up the place. And you won't be good to man nor beast lookin' the way you do. Ain't nobody gonna take on any street urchins. We need you to look proper."

"We don't have any money to be able to pay you."

"That's not my business," Maisie walked towards Lily, took the ragged hem of her dress, and began to tug it over her head. The material was flimsy and ripped easily. Lily's protests had Trixie shoving Maisie back, and Maisie snarled, advancing on Trixie with her fists clenched. The fist was drawn back but was held back when a bejewelled hand wrapped around her forearm.

"No time for that, Maisie. I told you to get these girls sorted – I came to see what was taking you so long," Stella calmly stated.

Maisie twisted her arm out of the hold, scowling at Trixie. "She won't do as she's told."

Stella's hawk-like gaze swung to Trixie. She sighed, her hands going to her narrow waist. "Now, what's the problem?"

"She was trying to take our clothes! These are all we have. What is this place?" The geyser of questions erupted. "Who are those children? What do you all do here? Why do you need me and my sister? Why did my sister *leave*?" The last question was squeaked out as tears filled her eyes and her throat tightened.

A quizzical brow arched above her left eye. "Have you quite finished?"

Trixie's lips rolled inwards, and she gave a small nod.

"Did you notice the others in there? What were they wearing?" Stella blinked at her, until Trixie felt compelled to answer.

"Nice clothes," she replied in a small voice.

"I'm not in the habit of stealing clothing off the backs of children, and I clothed everyone in there – in fact, everyone who lives under my roof wears clothes that I have bought. Angel included. Now, your dresses will be replaced with something more fitting," Stella lifted a finger to stem the next question as Trixie opened her mouth. "Save it! Wash, dress, eat... and then you and I will talk. Do we have an accord?"

Trixie took a moment to think. A quick glance down at the brown cloth that was once grey – and Lily wore a matching one that had once been Angela's and then hers. Her belly growled, reminding her that it had been days since she'd last manage to scavenge a morsel of food for them both. Lily blinked up at her, full of blind trust. At that moment, she knew that it fell onto her shoulders to save them both. Their mother had died, their father and then their sister had abandoned them. Trixie would do whatever she could to look after Lily.

It's not much of a choice but it'll be better than the workhouse...

With George's words echoing in her mind, Trixie nodded.

~

TRIXIE STARED at the blank piece of paper in front of her, the unfamiliar weight of an ink pen in her hand, and she shook her head. "I don't know how to write my name." She waited for the mockery to reach her from across the desk where Stella sat, but instead, the woman merely shrugged.

"Then we need to remedy that as soon as we can," She took the pen back and set it on top of the scarred table that she was using as a desk. "Lizzie is usually our resident teacher, but she's currently… detained at Her Majesty's pleasure. No matter, I can probably teach you some things myself. Your father… he didn't send you to school?"

Trixie shook her head. "He worked and then after my Ma passed, he spent his time in the White Lion, spending his coin until he lost that job. Then he was gone,"

Stella's thin lips twisted sardonically. "That, at least, matches the guff your sister fed me when I first met her. I should be impressed that she managed to keep a secret such as that one – not many people get things past me but, I don't mind admitting, she took me in hook, line, and sinker," She set the pen in a drawer at the front of the table, with her elbows on the top, she rested her chin on top of her linked fingers. "I won't make the same mistake again,"

"What do you want with me and my sister?" Trixie held the steady gaze.

True to her word, they'd been washed with soap and her hair was all soft and floaty. They had been given clean clothing that had fitted, though not very well. Maisie had mumbled that it would have to do. Then they'd been led to a huge room where more children must have arrived during their bath time, and they'd all sat in long trestle tables, the noise of so many children in one room had been thunderous. Lily had gobbled up the stew, dribbling the thin gravy down the front of her new dress whereas Trixie had worried about what was to come and picked at her food. When Lily had swiped her portion, Trixie had freely given it up for her. If Angela and her father had taught her one thing – it was that there was no such thing as a free ride in this life.

Maisie had assigned them a bed each, though Trixie knew that Lily would want to share hers. When Trixie had voiced this to Maisie, the older girl had shrugged and walked off. Everyone had been sent to bed as darkness settled over the high windows. Trixie had been curled up into a ball, Lily's soft slumbering breath tickling her ear when Maisie had summoned her, leading her through the building and up the spiral iron staircase that she'd seen Stella use when they'd arrived. The older woman had been seated at her desk and had handed Trixie the pen.

Now, Stella tilted her head, her red hair curling in wisps to frame her face. "I want you to work for me," she replied as if it was obvious.

"Doing what?"

"Does it matter to you?"

Trixie pictured the maids that she'd seen outside when they'd been talking to George and the many girls that had filled the room, oblivious to the newcomers. All had been well-fed, clean, and chatty. Many had read books before the dormitory lights had been extinguished.

"Is it what Angela did for you?"

A bubble of laughter rose in Stella's throat, and she extended a hand, snapped her fingers. George materialised into the pool of light from the desk lamp which gave Trixie a start – she hadn't seen him lurking in the shadows. She looked now and saw two other men hunkered against the walls, silently still as they watched the exchange. George handed Stella a pipe, added tobacco then lit it for her before he melted into the shadows once more. "What your sister did for me," she sucked on her pipe, smoke curled from her lips. "Maybe, one day you will. Who knows? She was the best I had – *was*." She took another drag, snuffled out a mirthless laugh as she sat back in her chair and contemplated the young girl across from her. "Maybe you'll be better, Trixie. But you will work for me, or you'll be in the river," she leaned forward as her eyes hardened. "Where she will be when I catch up with her."

Alarm gnawed at her insides. She pictured Lily's peaceful face, her cheeks red from the belly full of food, and pressed on before her bravery deserted her. "I know that you're angry with Angela – Angel," she corrected, "but I didn't know about this life that she led. She paid the rent; she went out to work. That's all we knew. We had to try and find work on the market, anywhere we could. Perhaps I should be angry with her, too. After all, it's her fault I'm here – she left us as well." She thought about the day Angela had left and realised now that she had tried to tell them to leave – *you shouldn't stay here....* She had known then that Stella would come looking.

Stella's eyes narrowed against the smoke that hazed the air around her, her lips thinning, though she remained mute.

"I have something to ask, though,"

"You want to bargain with me?" Stella's voice turned as hard as her stare.

Trixie swallowed, bobbed her head twice. "I will do whatever you ask me to do. Whatever it is you do here, I will do...without question," She knew what some women had to do to earn a couple of pennies. She'd been out on the streets at night, she'd seen the drunken men rutting behind a woman and knew that that was where babies came from.

Stella tossed back her head and laughed. "You will do that anyway, you brazen little madam!"

Trixie stepped forward, placed her hands on the desk, her eyes pleading. "I will. I won't run away, like Angel. I'll work for you, Stella. I will be better than Angela – than any of the girls that you have here."

"Is that so?" She quirked a brow in question, sent a look to the huge man behind her. "And what do I have to do in return?"

"You give Lily an honest job. Teach her the letters – and to write! She can clean or be a maid – I saw the girls leaving here today in a maid's uniform. She could do that," Trixie said enthusiastically, "Please. I beg of you. She is a child, and everyone has left her. I will do anything; you just leave my sister out of whatever business you have here."

Stella cleared her throat and took another drag on her

pipe as amusement shone in her eyes. "I don't believe I have ever met anyone quite as bold as you, child. Are you not frightened of me?"

"Of course," Trixie answered honestly.

Stella gave a throaty little laugh. "Good – I haven't quite lost my touch just yet then," She tapped the pipe into an ashtray, crushed the embers under it, and set it down as she considered the young girl. "I must be crazy, after what your sister did but you seem like a bright girl. I need quick minds and fast thinkers. For your boldness alone, I will agree to this. But," the sharp tone froze Trixie's jubilant smile into place. "If you once refuse to co-operate with any job, I will happily drown you both – with my own hands. Her first – and you will watch. Understand?"

CHAPTER 4

$\mathcal{T}$rixie

"SHOULDN'T you be in bed, little miss?"

The scream trapped in Trixie's throat, and she whirled on the deep gruff voice from near the door. George let the door swing to behind him, a smile playing around his lips as he walked further into the scullery.

"I… I," Trixie stuttered as her inert mind tried to come up with an excuse as to why she'd broken one of the cardinal rules in the sleeping hall. They weren't allowed to leave their beds. "I can't sleep," she decided to go with the truth instead, her heart returning to normal when she saw George instead of the stern Lizzie or got a telling off from Maisie. She'd never seen Stella here overnight and so guessed that she must reside elsewhere.

His warm eyes met hers. "Nervous about tomorrow? It's your first job, isn't it?"

Trixie bobbed her head once. "I don't think that I can do it, George. Stealing is wrong… lying is wrong,"

He pulled a chair out from the kitchen table, scarred, and covered in debris still from supper. "Not all of us have the opportunity to be able to decide what's right and wrong, Trixie," he said in a low voice as he leaned his elbows on top of the table. "Stella, she takes in kids off the streets, gives them the chance of a better life."

Trixie's brows knitted together, and she glanced at the door to ensure that it was shut. "She calls it a game, but it's not a game. It's stealing. It's tricking people, and taking…"

"From people who can afford it more than we can," George interrupted her.

"What if I get caught? I don't want to go to prison. Lizzie told us what happens there… it sounds horrible!" she retorted, then had to temper her tone when he lifted a finger to his lips. The door remained closed, and she sighed. "I don't want to do it,"

"You made a promise to Stella, remember? That night in her office? That she would educate Lily in exchange for you doing exactly what she wanted. Hasn't she kept her word?"

Trixie lowered her head as she acknowledged his words. She'd made an agreement with the devil, it seemed. She had to commit crimes and work with the other children to shoplift, and pickpocket, and take without getting caught. Tomorrow, she was to go out into the streets and work as part of a team. In the beginning, it had seemed like a simple thing to do. She had learned the words that she had been given. She could write her name, and she could count the beds in the dormitory hall. Tomorrow, she had to put it all into practice.

"Is there any milk?"

She nodded and quickly fetched him some, set the cup down, and crossed back to the sink to get herself some water from the pail. "I didn't know that you slept here," she said into the silence. "In all the months I've been here, I've not seen you about at night,"

He wiped the milk off his top lip with the back of his hand. "That's normally when I have to work," he said. "You're going to be fine, Trix. I've been hearing good things about you,"

She turned to him; her curiosity piqued as to who had said what. "Really? It seems I'm always in trouble with someone," she said ruefully. "If Stella isn't threatening to drown Lily or me, Lizzie is slapping at my hands when holding the pen, or Maisie is yelling because… well, because she's Maisie."

"She's gone a bit above her station since she was in charge. She'll soon settle down again now that Lizzie is back,"

Trixie wasn't convinced but didn't want to contradict him. Since her first day, he'd always been pleasant, saving a quick wink for her as he passed through the building. She still wasn't sure what it was that he did for Stella.

"What's that?" she asked when she saw the small box in his hands.

The corner of his mouth tilted, and he waved her over. He lifted the lid and showed her a deck of cards. "Have you ever played?"

She shook her head, creeping closer to him for a better look. "What do you do with them?"

"Play games, or do tricks? You can play a game by yourself. My Pa taught me how to play," He held the cards up to her for a closer look. "Each card has a pattern printed on it, and they make up like a team. You can play games where you have to match the symbol, or you add up the different symbols. Some of them have faces on, see?" He showed her what he meant. Trixie giggled at the haughty-looking expression on the king and queen as they peered back at her.

"What's a trick?"

"Aah," he smiled and took out a single card, held it up. It had red diamond shapes dotted across it. "How's your counting coming? How many is there?"

Trixie's eyes darted across. "Seven,"

His smile deepened. "They're right, you are a quick study. Okay, take this card. You see it?"

"Of course," she laughed, "It's right there!"

His hands moved deftly, and he held his empty hand out, palm up. "Are you sure?"

Her eyes popped wide. "Where…? It was…"

"It's here," he said, and with a flick of his wrist, pulled the card out from behind her ear. Trixie gasped and

George laughed at the look of wonder on her face. "How did you do that?" she said, taking the card between her fingers and turning it over.

George slipped the card back into the deck, shuffled them quickly. "You like it?"

"Yes! It's magic!"

He set the cards down, his lips twitching. "Not really. It's called 'sleight of hand'. Your hands can move faster than a person can see. Comes in handy, especially when you're on the streets in a team."

She frowned, not sure what he meant.

"Do it again," she demanded, and he obeyed, again making the card vanish. She asked him to do it a third time, watching his hands carefully, and still, the card vanished, returning from behind her ear. Then she met his amused gaze. "Teach me how to do it?"

He scratched the side of his nose as he pretended to think about it. "Get me some more milk...and a cookie from the tin up there, then." And they got to work.

⁓

"CHESTNUTS! GET YOUR CHESTNUTS! PENNY A SCORE!"

The hawker's voice bellowed, joining into the cacophony of sounds that filled the streets. Horse's hooves clattered as cabs rattled along the streets. Trixie tried to walk as though she had every right to be there, as if she and the other two people she was with weren't about to commit a crime. How does an innocent person walk, she wondered, as her eyes darted about the cobbled streets.

Well-dressed ladies rubbed shoulders with the shabbier-clothed maids, smartly dressed gentlemen strode with purpose. In between them, small children in threadbare clothes and bare feet darted around them, their wizened dark eyes staring out of grubby faces at the crowds about them. *That could have been me,* she thought now as she ran her damp palms down her smart navy dress that had little white flowers on it. She even had a matching blue ribbon in her hair. Lizzie had told her that they always made sure that their girls were better dressed so that they drew less attention when in shops. If they appeared like they had money, then shopkeepers wouldn't be quite so observant of them.

Trixie found herself looking for those with nefarious plans, looking for those like her, who had nimble fingers. She'd watched Maisie working; she'd seen Mary, Betty, Evie pull out a handkerchief and a coin purse without the person even knowing that they had been robbed. Today, it was her turn to join the team.

Coffee wafted from a stall, and copper pots gleamed in the light as they walked towards the market square. Costermongers called out their wares, and the market stalls were packed tightly in by the crowds of shoppers out to enjoy the dry weather.

Lizzie ducked her head down to Trixie's. "Get into position, you know what to do,"

Trixie pasted on a smile and hoped she looked more confident than how she felt. Lizzie was to appear as if she was an escort for the young women and was dressed in a long black skirt and starched white shirt with a buttoned-up collar. Evie and Trixie parted ways and merged into the crowds. Trixie's eyes tracked the shoppers, selecting and discarding her target, jostled about as adults barged past her. She saw Lizzie who indicated with her chin and Trixie followed the direction of her pointed gaze. She saw two women, clearly related, though one was much older. *Mother and daughter.*

The younger of them opened her mouth and brayed like a donkey as they strolled arm in arm, oblivious to those about them. Trixie sent a nod to Lizzie, swallowing down on the fizzing meal that she'd eaten that morning. She wiped her palms again, running through the instructions that Lizzie had snapped out on the carriage ride into the city. *Don't make it too obvious... Act natural... Be charming.... And if all hell breaks loose, run!* She wanted to run now, far away, but knew that she had no other choice than to follow through with her orders. After all, this is what she had been training to do since she had struck a deal with Stella. And there was Lily to consider.

Her sister remained unaware of what Trixie had been tasked to do. Lily was safely secure in the building with the rest of the children who were too small to do much just yet. Like the others, they all thought Stella was their fairy godmother – her actions inspired complete devotion to her by the children. Lily even wanted to start school. Lizzie caught Trixie's eye again, the pointed look getting more stern looking the further the women advanced into the square. Trixie shrugged a *what-do-you-want-me-to-do* look when the women stopped at a stall and she quickly walked up behind them, hovered, and waited as the older women pointed at a brooch on the black cloth that covered the stall.

"Do you a good deal," the market trader revealed a toothless grin to them, and she began to barter with him. Trixie tuned into the conversation, awareness prickling her skin as her pulse raced, pounding at her throat. She stepped up next to the woman, deliberately close so that when the woman turned, she collided with Trixie and knocked her off her feet.

"Oh, golly!" The woman cried out when she whirled, reaching out to help Trixie up to her feet, "I didn't see you!"

"You should watch where you're going!" the daughter said, shaking her head.

Pink flooded Trixie's cheeks when real tears flooded her eyes and she covered her face, but not before she'd seen Lizzie behind the two women. "I'm sorry!" Trixie sobbed, the sweet release of giving into her tears easing her anxiety. "I didn't see you!"

"Hush, now," the mother admonished, "Are you okay? Have you hurt yourself?"

Trixie lowered her hands, catching the flash of green ribbon in Evie's hair as she crossed behind Lizzie, no doubt having whatever Lizzie had taken from the women passed to her. Evie's job was now to get out of the market square with the stolen goods whilst Trixie and Lizzie dealt with the aftermath of the ruse.

"Gertrude!" Lizzie admonished, her harsh cockney

accent now suddenly smoothed out. It amazed Trixie that she could alter her voice in such a way. "There you are! I lost you, I told you to stay by me. Why are you crying?"

"This lady knocked me down!"

The older woman gasped and babbled out an explanation and a hasty apology. "I'm terribly sorry. It was an accident."

"No harm," Lizzie told the woman and took hold of Trixie's hand, "no need to apologise. Come, Gertie, we need to get home. Your mother will be wondering where we've got to,"

"'Ere, do you want this or not?" The market trader asked them as they were walking away and the woman turned back to him, the incident seemingly out of her mind. Lizzie and Trixie had made it to the edge of the square when the cry of 'thief' went up from somewhere behind them. Trixie's sense went onto full alert, even as she had to trot to keep up with Lizzie's hurried strides, weaving down alleys, along back streets to where George and another waited, with the carriage door open, and Evie already inside.

"How'd it go?" George enquired idly.

Lizzie snorted. "This one thinks she's in a theatre, balling her eyes out on cue and wailing like a right little actress." Her tone sounded disgusted though when she looked at George, he was grinning and shot her a wink that made her own lips twitch.

"Take those goods," Lizzie pointed at the two coin purses, a scarf, and a watch that one of them must have pickpocketed whilst Trixie was dithering around. "And get them to where they need to go."

Trixie gaped at Evie as she hopped down out of the carriage and brushed at some lint on her skirt. "We're not leaving?"

"You think that's enough to feed all those mouths at the warehouse? No, you snivelling idiot, we're not. We go again. And this time, try better."

～

FELIX

"YOU TURN UP HERE, looking like a wild man. It's enough to scare the wits from any normal person, let alone a woman of a certain age!" Frank Huxley's voice held a tone of censorship that Felix hadn't heard before.

"There aren't many barbers in the deepest Indies, brother, and I can't afford to travel with the luxury of a valet. Besides, I've been a little busy to concern myself with grooming to please your ruddy housekeeper," Andrew Huxley's retort sounded bored.

"All I'm saying is a little warning of your visit would have been appreciated, Andrew. Poor Mrs. Akerman, no wonder she's so flustered." Frank Huxley busied himself making tea off the tray that his housekeeper had set down with a snap, inciting a mocking laugh from his wayward youngest sibling.

Andrew Huxley appeared unmoved by the disturbance

that his sudden and late arrival to the rectory had caused. He sat indolently in the seat; fingers laced across his belly. "And here was me thinking a man of the cloth would welcome one of his sheep – or whatever it is you call the congregation these days. I'm afraid I'm a little out of touch with what's been going on," he nodded towards the small child perched at the end of the sofa. "My point being *that*. I suppose Mother would be pleased that at least one of us has had a child if nothing else."

Felix kept his head bowed, trying to look at this gregarious stranger in his bizarre clothing without being noticed. The man was tall, and slender, with a thick dark beard and scruffy hair was tied at the nape of his neck into a tail. He had on dusty sand-coloured field boots from which material spiralled up his legs and stopped at his knees, where the material ballooned out. He wore a short linen jacket in the same cream colour as his trousers and a smock shirt that was open at the neck, revealing leather thongs tied there that had peculiar talismans hanging from them.

"Don't talk about him like he's not here, Andrew. He's neither deaf nor stupid. The boy needed a home, and I had the room. In fact, Felix has been a delight and an honour to share this house with. He's doing well in his education. He has plans to be a doctor one day."

Andrew Huxley's bushy brows met as he sent a surprised look at his brother, and then to the boy. "That right? I would have thought you'd have wanted him to follow you, make an oath to believe in some paper, not explore science."

Frank Huxley tutted his annoyance. "You're being deliberately inflammatory, Andrew, and I won't rise to the bait. Here's your coffee,"

Andrew reached for the cup, holding it up in his outstretched hand as he grinned unrepentantly at his oldest brother. "Are we making it Irish tonight? I've had a long journey, brother dear."

The lid of the flask rattled, and their attention was on the alcohol, so Felix took a moment to study the reverend's youngest brother. He'd heard snippets about him, knew that he travelled extensively, and was looked upon with a degree of both embarrassment and confusion by Frank and his family. Felix ducked his gaze when Andrew turned and looked at him.

"What's on your mind, boy?"

"N– nothing, sir." Felix stammered, pulling at the material of his breeches. Frank slipped his flask back into his hip pocket and sat in his usual armchair next to the hearth.

"You keep watching me like I'm about to sprout another head. Frank says you like to learn, and you won't learn anything if you don't ask, so what is it?"

Felix felt mortification score his cheeks red under the attention from both men. Frank tried to come to his defence, but Andrew stopped him and pressed Felix for an answer. "You dress funnily," Felix said in a rush, "Why?"

The beard moved and Felix saw the teeth flash in a grin through the scruff. "Because, where I've been, it's hot – too hot for woollen coats and top hats. The humidity is enough to make you melt – this?" he tugged at the collar of his coat – "it's designed to absorb a man's sweat and keep the bugs from eating me alive,"

Felix's eyes grew wide. "Bugs? Like bed bugs?"

Andrew nodded. "Similar, though different to anything that you would have seen. I have brought some back to put on display at one of the exhibitions in London. Lots of insects – many strange and wonderful critters that would take a bite out of anything in their way,"

Felix watched him, fascinated, as he discussed being devoured by something in such an offhand manner. "Can I see them?"

"Certainly, young man. When the display is up, we can make a trip." Andrew finished his drink and dragged the back of his hand across his whiskers.

Frank passed his brother a handkerchief and pointed to the moisture on his hand. "I'm trying to educate the boy on etiquette and manners, Andrew. Respectably dry your mouth, please."

Andrew grunted but did as he was told.

"What's that symbol on your neck?" Felix had slid along the sofa and was watching the other man intently, buoyed by his candour. "Like the cross but round on top? I've not seen that before? Do the bugs pray to the Lord, too?"

Andrew chuckled. "I don't think animals have such free thought as to think about a deity, my boy. Probably just where they can next eat, or build a home, or breed more of them. And this?" He held up the symbol, blackened through wear, "is an ankh. It was carved for me by a friend from a tree that only grows next to a particular river. It is a symbol, just like your cross for Christianity, but it is from an ancient civilisation. I wear it for luck and long life,"

Felix tilted his head as he considered the man. "Was your friend like Christopher Columbus?"

Andrew sent an appreciative glance at Frank, leaned forward so his elbows were on his knees to look more earnestly at the boy. "You know about the writings of Columbus?"

"I read about him, in a book in the library. He discovered lands that no one had seen before."

Andrew nodded. "Do you have that book? I could maybe show you some things that I've seen – if you'd like to hear about it?"

Felix shot to his feet, "Oh, yes, sir! Can I, Frank? Can I show Andrew?"

"It's getting late, Felix. Aren't you tired? We have to visit the alms house tomorrow, hand out our contributions and hear prayers there."

"Not the least bit tired!" He didn't mind visiting the poor people, but what he loved most was reading about adventures of far-off lands.

"The boy needs an education better than he can get at any alms house, Frank. The world is a marvellous playground for his inquisitive mind to explore."

"I have a responsibility to him," Frank said mildly to his brother. "It's hardly fair to keep him up discussing the trials and tribulations of Columbus when we have made commitments to the community."

"So, you'll be an hour late in the morning?" Andrew reasoned.

"I'll get up on time, and not be sleepy! I promise!" Felix could feel the reverend's resolve wavering and sprinted from the room when he was given his nod of sighing resignation.

CHAPTER 5

$\mathscr{E}$

$\mathcal{T}$rixie

I<small>T WAS</small> the loud crash that jolted her from a deep sleep. Trixie lay awake, her heart in her throat as her ears tuned into the screaming silence. The muffled cursing roused her into an upright position. Pale moonlight shone through the high-up windows, its silvery light slanting across the beds that were crammed into the large hall so that she could see the shape of Maisie as she slipped through the darkness and out into the entrance part of the building. Lizzie's rules were that you weren't allowed to leave your bed. She knew this because Maisie reiterated it nightly to the group when she coordinated the bedtime routine. Trixie hesitated for a second but when she recognised the hoarse shout, she followed Maisie through the door like a whippet.

"What are you doing?" Maisie hissed at her when they all turned to the sound of Trixie's gasp. George was hanging between two of Stella's henchmen. His left side was soaked with blood and his head lolled around on his shoulders as they lugged him towards the scullery, his shoes trailing on their tips behind him. "Get back to bed!" Maisie lifted a hand and pointed at the door, but Trixie's attention was on George. She batted Maisie's hand out of the way as she followed the trio of men in time to see them drop him unceremoniously into a chair.

"Where's Lizzie?" The one they called Billy gasped.

"Asleep, probably," muttered Trixie. She didn't need to ask what had happened. Judging by the state of the three of them, it would be best that she didn't know. Instead, she filled a bucket with water, grabbed some rags and the cooking sherry. "Maisie, boil some water. Do we have any whisky anywhere?"

"You don't get to tell me what to do," Maisie groused and tried to stand in Trixie's way.

Billy straightened up, sharp eyes on her and he lit a cigarette, inhaled sharply. "You know what you're doing, girl? Lizzie normally bandages us up,"

Sweat mixed in with the dried blood on George's face, dripping off his chin. His one eye was swollen shut, and his split lip oozed. Trixie dipped one of the cloths into the water and she stepped up to him, assessing the damage.

"This needs a needle, not bandages," Trixie said as an aside. "Does Lizzie have any?"

"You need to stop interfering and get out of here," Maisie tried to pull Trixie back, and again was shaken off.

A bottle of whisky was set on the table by the other man, John. His scarred face normally terrified Trixie, but her focus was on fixing George. "Here," he said. "Go get Lizzie," He instructed Maisie, "let her alone for a moment."

The door banged as Maisie slammed out of the kitchen. "Hold this here like this," Trixie pressed the damp cloth on George's face, holding his head up.

"That's not what I do,"

Trixie tilted her head to glare at the gruesome-looking man. "Are you scared of a little blood? Just stop being a baby and do as I ask. Please," she added when he stared at her.

Billy snatched the cloth out of her hands, aiming a dark look at John. He stood next to George, who moaned softly when the cold compress was applied to his swelling face. Next, she peeled back the vest, unbuttoned his shirt, and pushed the material back. A slit in his belly oozed a steady flow of blood. Trixie picked up the whisky and tugged on the cork, but had to hand it to John, who did as she silently requested with an arch of her brow, and he gave her back the bottle with the cork removed.

"How old are you?" John asked her.

She poured the whisky on the cut. "Nine now," she replied absently, pressing the cloth to the wound.

"How do you know about this?"

"My Pa was a drinker. The woman who lived next door was a healer, though she had to use vinegar, not whisky. Many a time my Pa had a beating,"

The door burst inwards, and Lizzie appeared, gas light

aloft and a dark scowl on her face. She took in the scene as she set the lamp down and planted her hands on her hips. "Do I dare ask?"

Trixie met and coolly held the woman's gaze. "He's my friend," she said simply.

Lizzie rolled her eyes and took down a rusty tin from a shelf, flipping the lid off it. "What happened?"

"We got surrounded, had a disagreement when trying to make a collection. They didn't wanna pay," Billy shrugged, "You know how it can be sometimes,"

"Did he hit his head?"

"It's not bleeding," Trixie replied when Billy and John just looked at each other. "I checked."

Trixie moved out of the way as Lizzie nudged her back and set to work. The two men did as they were instructed and laid George out on the table, and he groaned loudly. The sound was encouraging – dead people didn't moan.

"He needs a doctor. Go and fetch one. Bring him here and don't take no for an answer," she said. "Trixie, stoke the fire. He needs to be kept warm, then come here and help me." Lizzie dispatched with George's shirt more firmly than Trixie had, exposing his chest. Bruises – both fresh and ones faded green dotted the skin.

"Is he going to be okay?" Trixie murmured as she stood at the table, George's battered face turned towards hers, his brows drawn together.

Lizzie grunted at her. "Move the light, hold it there," She hooked the thread in, started passing the needle into the skin. "You know that Maisie is in charge when I'm not about," She was focused on her task, her tone as brisk as it always was.

Trixie sighed. "Yes."

"And that we have a hierarchy here. You earn your place; you get your respect."

"Yes, but he's my friend. He's been the only one…"

Lizzie's hands stilled. "The only one?"

"I know that you have all helped me," Trixie amended at the glower from the older woman. "It's just that George…" She shrugged, not knowing how else to explain how he'd become like a surrogate older brother to her in the half-year since she'd arrived. "Angela left; George was there." She replied eventually.

"Snip this thread. The scissors are in my tin," Lizzie washed her hands in the bucket by their feet, examined the cut near his eye, tutted. "This fool needs to learn to move faster,"

Trixie cut the cotton, put the needle in the tin after she'd washed it, just like the old healer woman had shown her.

The ruckus outside of the door signalled the return of the others. John and Billy pushed the doctor through the door, his black bag clutched to his chest. He blinked owlishly, his eyes huge behind the wired spectacles. Trixie wondered what he must have thought about being dragged out in the dead of the night, and being greeted by a bloody and unconscious man, a grouchy matron, and an orphan. Whatever his thoughts, he shook off the hands of the two men and crossed to the table.

"You can go, Trixie," Lizzie told her. Trixie thought

THE QUEEN OF THIEVES

about arguing but as she was pushed further to the back of the room, she knew that she would just get in the way. She paused at the door to find Lizzie watching her quietly. Lizzie nodded and, for the first time, her lips quirked at the corners into a small smile.

Trixie slunk through the hall, into the dormitory, and climbed back into bed. Her heart was full of fears for her friend, but for the first time, she felt like maybe she was starting to fit in here.

∼

TRIXIE WASN'T sure at what point the trick had gone wrong. One minute, she had selected her target: two men wearing clothing that she'd marked as gentry, guffawing as they'd strolled along the busy street towards a street fair.

They'd had cover, and the three had fanned out, melting into the crowded street. This time, Maisie had been the one to stop them both to ask for directions, creating a bottle neck on the pavement where they'd stood. Evie had picked their pockets, though just as Trixie had passed behind her and taken the items, a hand had clamped down on Trixie's shoulder.

After having lived like this for months, it had become more of a game to her. Maybe she'd grown cocky, more daring. Maybe she'd slowed up. She'd justified her feelings of remorse by telling herself it was how she survived. It was how she fed herself, it was how Lily was sat in a classroom in a school now, learning to read and writing out her name. They were part of a misguided family, and she was beginning to like it. She'd almost given up on the foolish notion that she could run away.

As she turned and looked up into the scornful, pitted face of a man in a blue police uniform, her insides turned watery and cold fear turned her face to stone. She longed to look for Maisie, for Evie, but didn't want to give them away. They were to run. Those were the rules. You didn't look back. Instead, she held the contemptuous stare of the man as he pressed his reddened face towards hers.

"Not so fast! You come with me!" His pudgy hand closed around the top of her arm like a vice, and he dragged her behind him as he flagged down her two marks. "Excuse me, sirs – have you lost anything of value here today?"

The two well-dressed men from the country turned in surprise, the one adjusting his spectacles to peer at the pair. "I beg your pardon?"

The officer hauled Trixie up in front of them, his fingers biting deeper. "I saw a pickpocket's trick happening to you, from where I was stood in the doorway over there. Have you got your coin purse? Your watch?"

Trixie pulled at her arm in vain. She altered her voice, changed her accent, as she had seen Lizzie and the others do, many a time. "You let me go! I'm no pickpocket!"

"Do you think I came down in the last shower, Miss?" the police officer snarled at her. "I saw it with my own eyes, I did!"

"You're right," the shorter of the two cried, patting his

pockets, his eyes bulging in horror. "I've been robbed! What have you done with my stuff, you thieving critter!"

Trixie sucked in a breath, drawing herself up. "I assure you, I'm no critter, you impudent toad. Now, let me go! Don't you know who I am?"

The shorter man's brows climbed up his head. "Well, I never heard such language," he breathed, "from a child, no less! Where is my money?"

The policeman shook her, oblivious to the crowd that was gathering about them to watch the spectacle. "Hand over the stuff, and then I'm taking you down the station. Scum like you deserve to hang, preying on decent people."

"That's what I'm telling you," She spread her hands, sending him a disdainful look, "I don't have anything. Is there anything in my hands? No! Do I have a bag, or any pockets? No! I don't know what you think you saw, but you got it wrong. Now, unhand me or my father will have your job!"

She could tell her haughty tone and stature had him thrown as he hesitated. His eyes scanned her simple dress. He swallowed and was less certain when he said, "Your father? Where is he then?"

"Down the street," she pulled again on her arm "We got separated in the crowds, and now, thanks to you, I am lost to him. He will be furious when I tell him it was you that put bruises on his only child."

The policeman released her. "Well, where is his money? His watch? I saw the girl stop them, I seen it coming... You walked right behind them...". His lips thinned and he patted the sides of her hips, drawing a shocked gasp from the crowd, "I know what I saw!"

"I say, dear man, you... that isn't right," the shorter man interjected, distaste twisting his face, "You cannot mishandle a young lady so. It simply... isn't right," he tugged out his handkerchief, dabbed at his top lip. "She clearly doesn't have the items. I think you have a case of mistaken identity here,"

Trixie pulled her arm free, rubbed at the area as tears filled her eyes on cue. "Thank you, sir – and I apologise for my language. Can I go?" she took advantage of his momentary confusion and, without waiting for an answer, slipped through the circular crowd to make her escape.

CHAPTER 6

$\mathcal{T}$rixie

TRIXIE BROKE out of the other side of the crowd and, without looking back, began to run. She rounded the corner and drew up short when she saw Maisie stood there.

"Are you waiting for me?" she asked, surprised. They were meant to run. If something went wrong, you were on your own.

Maisie's eyes darted behind her, where the crowd still gathered. She jerked her head, and grabbed Trixie's hand, they took off at a run, pumping their hands and legs in unison. By the time they reached the meet-up point, both girls were blowing hard.

Billy's brows climbed up his head as he opened the

door to the cab. "I was about to give up on you," he groused, "Evie said you got caught, Trixie."

'She did," panted Maisie, as she run up the steps and flopped down on the bench next to Evie. "But a little thing like yelling at a copper sorted out that problem,"

"That so?" Billy shut the door behind him, admiration in his tone. He sent her a wink before he moved away from the door.

Trixie sat down, her heart thundering in her chest, her arm throbbing from where the policeman had held her. Her eyes danced between the two girls sat opposite her as she tried to get her breathing back under control. The carriage jerked and she braced herself on her hands. Maisie smirked at her, and Trixie's lips twitched in response. Laughter, nervous yet releasing bubbled up inside her, until she was folded forward, gasping for breath once more.

"Trixie," Maisie chuckled, "I have no idea where all that comes from, but it was brilliant! His face when you called him a toad! I thought he was going to pop a button!"

"What happened?" Evie asked.

"Trixie got collared, demanded to be released as they had the wrong person!"

"You yelled at the peelers?"

"And the man we robbed! Where did you drop the stuff?" Maisie wiped at her tears.

Trixie frowned, her smirk widening to a grin as she shook her sleeve and the watch dropped out into her lap.

She reached into her waist band, pulled out the coin purse, set it on top of the watch. "Who said I dropped it?"

Maisie gaped at her, wondrous eyes meeting hers. "How did you...? He had you before Evie had finished? And who's is that?"

With a flourish, Trixie held up the leather purse that she'd pulled from the policeman's coat and dangled it in the air. "That'll teach that mutton shunter to put his hands on me, won't it? It's what it cost him for putting bruises on me."

Maisie shook her head. "You even had me convinced, Trixie!"

Her lips curved and she leaned back, feeling smug. "What the eyes don't see..."

~

"You robbed the peeler, as he was trying to arrest you?" Smoke trailed from the deep red lips of Stella, her dark eyes contemplating Trixie from across the desk. The watch and two purses sat in between them both. Stella tapped the ash from the end of her cigarette and angled her head.

Trixie wasn't sure if it was appreciation or loathing that sparked in the other woman's expression as she nodded mutely at the question.

"She squared up to him," Maisie supplied helpfully, "I saw it. Told him her Pa was going to take his job if he didn't let her go, too!"

Stella pursed her lips. "Maisie said he patted you down. How did you hide them without him noticing?"

Trixie's eyes slid to where George lounged indolently to Stella's right. "It's all about distraction," she mumbled.

Stella stubbed out the cigarette. She snapped her fingers and pointed at the loot, sending a look at George. "This shouldn't be here. If anyone comes looking for it here, we'll all be done for. Take it and fence it, as fast as you can,"

George was grinning from ear to ear as he leaned across the table, the scar on his lip pulled white. "Sure thing, boss lady," he scooped up the items and winked at Trixie, who ducked her head to hide her smile. He'd shown her how to do what she did. It was thanks to him that she was able to bluff her way out of the situation.

Stella's nails drummed a beat on her desk as she stared at Trixie. "You took a risk. I still don't know how you did it, considering that filthy pig felt you up, too."

Trixie opened her mouth to correct the older woman, but Maise nudged her slightly and she closed her mouth again.

"I also don't know what's changed between the two of you," a finger waggled between her and Maisie, "but it seems to be working. You can't go back out on the streets," She stated, eyes on Trixie. "The police will be on the lookout for you, now. Your card will be marked and, if that copper has anything about him, he'll have a description up and all my kids will be getting watched. You made a mistake, not to have seen him in the first place. You were told to always check the vicinity."

Trixie wanted to defend herself, the victorious bubble inside her deflating as Stella pointed out everything that she had done wrong.

"None of that stuff should have come back here. Maisie shouldn't have waited for you. I could have lost two girls today – and now we can't work that part of town until the peelers move on to someone else," She stood, the emerald green of her dress swishing around her feet as she rounded the table. "You messed up, ya hear me?"

Trixie lowered her gaze, nodding miserably, as her mind spiralled. "Are you going to throw me out?"

Stella perched on the corner and folded her arms. "I should do, but I won't." She held up a finger and Trixie's relief was short-lived. "Though you're not staying around here. We need to get you out of the town. You can go and work one of the con's out in the country,"

Lily. "But–"

"No 'but's' allowed. You brought this upon yourself. We'll sort you a reference. You leave in the morning,"

Trixie stared, her eyes tracking her boss as she walked back to her chair, seemingly pleased with her decision. Normally, Trixie kept her emotions hidden, not wanting to show how much she wanted something in case it was taken away from her. She'd learned that after years of living with a drunken father who had a spiteful streak but now, she couldn't hold back the fear.

"What about my sister? I can't leave here. I promised her that I wouldn't leave her. I can't break my word to her – I *promised!*"

Stella sat down and lifted her shoulders, her tone indifferent. "Then, maybe next time you'll follow the rules."

~

"You're going to be fine," George handed her the battered suitcase that she'd been told to carry with her. It was empty, save for a book and a coat that had been pilfered off someone. Nerves zigged along her veins, and she wiped her sweaty palms down the plain blue skirt she wore. The steam trains huffed and hissed at the platform edges, the billowing smoke filling the station as the crowds eddied around the pair. George leaned closer so that only she could hear his words. "Anyone that can bluff her way out of a collar from the peelers will go a long way,"

Trixie tried to take comfort in his words, though misery etched her face when he straightened up. If she had only thought to get rid of the items, instead of gloating to Maisie, she wouldn't have been sent away. The memory of Lily's sobs squeezed her heart, and she looked to George with tear-filled eyes. "Will you look out for Lily? I'm worried about her,"

George ran a hand over her hair and nodded. "Course, I will. Don't you be fretting none. You got a job to do."

She scanned his face, her instructions floating through her mind. "I'm not sure I can… I'm usually part of a team…"

George dropped to his haunches in front of her. "Don't

you see what's happened here? You've been promoted, Trixie. Stella has seen potential in you."

Her eyes moved between his kind dark ones. This felt more like a punishment, but George has yet to lie to her.

"Most girls don't get to the big houses until they're twelve or older. Until they can pull a switch, or swipe some jewels, and slip out unnoticed. You got away from that copper by what's in here," he gently rapped his knuckles on her skull. "With talent and dexterity that takes years to learn. And the benefit is? No one will look at a kid. *That's* what Stella was thinking. You'll be okay. Now, be off with you," he straightened up and chucked her under the chin. "I got work to do and you have a train to catch."

Following her instinct, she wrapped her arms around George's middle and hugged him quickly before she weaved her way through the people and clambered aboard the train. She found a seat by the window, moving along the carriage with the strange scents of leather and tobacco filling her senses. She took her seat, lifting a hand to wave to George before he was obscured in the drifting puff from the train. She hugged the small case to her as she looked out at the many faces that milled about the platform. Absently, she picked out several marks in the crowd, knowing where they would keep their valuables. When had she become so adept at simply taking?

I have to be okay, for Lily's sake. She had had to pry her little sister off her this morning, and it had broken her heart hearing the sobs echo throughout the building as Trixie had had to walk away from her. Tears stung her eyes. For the first time in her life, she was all alone and had no clue how she would fare in the wider world, away from the hubbub of the city, from her family. From Lily.

A sharp whistle rented the air and with a metallic clank, the train jerked into life, chugging its way out of London and onto the next job.

~

FELIX

"NO TEARS, YOUNG MAN," Andrew chucked Felix under the chin, a rueful smile dancing about his bare lips. "We will be seeing each other again."

Felix blinked against the burning heat behind his eyes, trying in vain to do as he was told. "I know, sir,"

Frank slipped a hand over Felix's scrawny shoulders and squeezed. "I share his sentiment, brother dear. It's been grand having you at home for these last few months. The time went too fast, even for my liking," he shook the hand that Andrew held out. "Safe travels, and may the Lord keep you in His hands until we meet again."

"I'm sure that the Lord has better things to do with his time than to watch over an unrepentant wretch like me, but thank you, Frank." Andrew dropped to his haunches in front of Felix so that they were eye level. "Now then, Felix. I wanted to tell you that I have never enjoyed my stay in England as much as I have this time. I want you to carry on with your learning, keep reading and keep your mind open to new possibilities. Can you do that for me?"

"Yes, sir," Felix promised solemnly. He couldn't quite imagine not listening to the adventures of Andrew – the foreign places, and the things he had seen. "When you're home next, can we visit the exhibitions again?"

Andrew smiled. "Naturally. We must go and see what they have added to their collection in my absence," he reached inside his overcoat, pulled out a pouch. "I have something for you."

Felix took the item, tugged on the drawstring, and made a small intake of breath when he recognised what dropped into his hand. Felix lifted his startled gaze to Andrew's calm one. "Your ankh pendant!"

"And now it's your ankh pendant," he slid the leather string about the child's head.

"But won't your friend be cross that you gave it away?"

Andrew ruffled his hair fondly. "I'm sure he'll understand when I tell him that I gave it to my new friend back in England. You'll wear it as your good luck talisman?"

"I will," Felix promised, "thank you, Andrew."

"I shall pretend that you're not encouraging heathen views on an impressionable mind," Frank rebuked his brother softly.

"He can hide it behind the crucifix," Andrew straightened up and grinned. "He can believe in more than one system – it's worked well enough for me across the years. Stay healthy, brother dear. I'll see you in a year or so." Andrew walked towards the waiting carriage at the end of the garden.

Felix rubbed the smooth surface of the pendant, watching his new friend leave. Even though he'd been told not to, he couldn't hold back his tears. He felt like he'd been on a wonderful adventure with Andrew and his life would be empty without his vibrancy in it.

Frank patted him on the head. "And then there was just the two of us again," he murmured, lifted a hand in greeting as the cab disappeared. "Shall I ask Mrs Akerman to make us some tea?"

Felix nodded miserably, staring at the end of the drive. He longed to go with Andrew, to see for himself the magical places he'd spoken about. "I shall miss him,"

Frank steered him towards the front door. "I know. Funnily enough, I will, too. I don't think I've ever enjoyed Andrew being home as much before. Isn't that odd? I don't think I've paid quite so much attention to how he lives his life," he shut the door, rested a hand as a puzzled frown creased his brow. For a moment, he seemed lost in thought. He looked to Felix, unhappiness turning his mouth down. "How about some biscuits? I think today we deserve two each, just because."

CHAPTER 7

❧

*T*wo Years Later.

Trixie

"I want to be able to see my face shine on this floor, Mary. Wash it again. I won't have any of his Lordship's guests pass a judgement on this house! Master Peter's party will go off without a hitch. Get and do it again!" The old housekeeper, Mrs Martin, slammed from the room. Trixie sighed, dipping the brush into the bucket and she dropped to the floor, applying the bristles to the tiles once more.

"How can you see a face in slate?" Beth grumbled from across the room, lifting her bucket with the ashes as she picked her way over the damp floor. She used the back of her hand to push back on the lock of mousy brown hair that tumbled over her forehead, stopped near to where Trixie was working.

Trixie dipped for more water, sloshed it on the floor. She was always called Mary on a job, having a common first name meant that she was used to being called it, and paid attention whenever she heard it. She hadn't been called Trixie in a while "Maybe Mrs Martin is so ugly, she broke every looking-glass and doesn't actually know what she looks like,"

Beth giggled, her grubby hand covering the crooked teeth that flashed. "Oh, Mary, you would get flogged if she heard you talk that way."

Trixie gave a dismissive shrug. "She'd have to catch me first," she muttered. When the door swung open, her heart skipped a beat, but it was the other thief that she was collaborating on this posting with, instead of the bloated housekeeper's face, that appeared in the doorway. She wore the black and white uniform of a maid. Trixie knew her as Anna, though she highly doubted that was her real name.

"What are you looking so guilty about, Mary," she asked, shooting a dark look at the younger Beth so that she scurried away for more hot water. She followed Beth to the door, checked the hallway was empty before turning back and closing the door, leaning on it as she skewered Trixie with a look. "I've had a letter from the top. She's making noises about what's taking us so long on this job,"

Of all the postings Trixie had had in the past two

years, Mrs Martin was possibly the most cantankerous of all housekeepers that she'd come across. She was meant to be a chambermaid here – but, quite quickly, plans had been messed up when Mrs Martin kept changing her duties and Trixie was suddenly on restricted access to the bedrooms and study. And no amount of charm had worked on Mrs Martin, or the duke who employed them all.

"I'm working on it," Trixie went back to cleaning the floor, keeping her voice down. "I know what I need to do, don't worry yourself about it."

"I do worry!" Anna hissed, leaning toward her for emphasis. "I cannot bear the old bat in charge, and I'm sick of boiling cabbage, and emptying slop buckets full of that old man's…" She stopped when footsteps echoed in the hallway beyond the door. She waited until it went silent again. "Stella wants us out by the end of the week – with the job completed, or she said to tell you that the deal is over."

Trixie sat back on her heels, dropped the brush into her bucket, uncaring of the water that sloshed out onto the floor. She scrubbed her eyes with the heels of her hands. She hated this whole job, and she longed for the early days of when she'd first left London. It had been positively easy back then, compared to this job. The well-written references and her polite manners had endeared her to most employers, so that they were unaware that she was the one manipulating the butlers, the housekeepers, sometimes even the grouchy men of the house. A little sleight of hand, a little distraction…

The keys to the safe. Watches, gems as big as her fist, emptying bulging jewellery boxes, and cash. Simple jobs. She'd fled premises in the night wearing furs, pearls twisted around her neck. She always worked with another person, and they would meet her and then help facilitate her escape. They'd be a maid, or a groom, or a kitchen hand. They'd flee one way with the loot; she'd be moved on to the next place with a fresh reference, ready to blend in once more. But this job had been soured from the get-go.

"Did you hear me, girl? The deal? She said to say –"

"I heard!" Trixie snapped, firing a venomous look at Anna. She tempered her tone, knowing that she had to work with this woman or risk getting left behind. Though, in the two years that she'd been doing this, she was yet to have Stella dangle the deal she'd made about Lily over her head. In the wee hours of the morning, she longed to see Lily. She wrote to her, though Lily was forbidden from writing back, in case it gave her away. She shoved thoughts of her old life away, needing to focus on the job.

"If you weren't who you are…" Anna's face twisted in disdain. "Everyone sings your bleedin' praises, telling me how impressive you are – the one who has never failed on a job yet! Well, from where I'm stood, you ain't doing all that great now, are yer? Get in, get those bleedin' papers and let's get from 'ere!" Anna wrenched the door open and left the room, her clipped pace echoing away from the drawing room.

Trixie stifled a sigh, patting her tender hands on the

skirts of her uniform to dry them. The skin was red from the soda flakes and had cracked in between her fingers. She wanted to leave here as much as Anna did. The chemicals played havoc on her skin and her knees were sore from grubbing around the floors for most of the day. Mrs Martin was handy with whatever weapon she had to hand and thought nothing of clobbering the staff as they passed by her.

She just didn't know where these letters were that she'd been sent here to find. And she'd looked in drawers, in the bureau. No communication for the duke was to be found anywhere. She'd tried sneaking into the bed chambers but had come close to being caught on more than one occasion. She's always been careful not to be fired from a job before she'd completed her task. Holding up her end of the deal was what was keeping Lily safe and in school. She wondered what was so important that she was to intercept post this time, not diamonds or the fat sapphire that the Duchess wore often around her stout neck.

The door opened and was closed quickly as Beth slipped back through; her eyes as wide as saucers.

"Run, quick!" she whispered, "Peter is coming, and he's got the light of the devil in his eyes!"

Grateful for the forewarning, Trixie stood but wasn't fast enough as the door hit Beth in the back. She leapt forward out of the way, blushing beetroot red and bowed her head as Peter walked in. His gaze alighted upon Trixie, and he dismissed Beth with a wave, his eyes not moving.

"But, Your Grace, I have to wash…"

"Out, you wretch," he muttered, prowling towards Trixie, "Leave us alone."

Trixie saw Beth dip in a semblance of a curtsy on her periphery, as she held the rampant stare of the duke's only son. He was handsome, though his fervent stare and perpetual sneer meant that all the female staff was afraid of him.

"Hello, Mary," he purred.

Her oatmeal breakfast rolled nauseously in her belly, but she bobbed a curtsy and sent him a small smile. She wouldn't be rude to him, but he was another reason she hated this posting. "Good morning, Your Grace,"

"I thought about you a lot on my trip to London. Did you think about me?" He came to a halt a foot away from her, tilting his head as his eyes raked over her.

"Not really, Your Grace," she mimicked the head tilt. It was the truth. He bothered most of the staff, always the younger ones and he was sneaky about it. "I have a lot to do every day. It doesn't leave much room for other things in my head."

His lips curved up at the edges and he trailed a finger down her arm. "You're not scared of me, are you?"

She wanted to recoil, and it took everything in her not to tremble. She wanted to bolt but instinctively knew to hold her ground. "Why would I be scared of you, Your Grace?"

The finger moved to her chin. This time, she pulled her chin up and his grin spread, the dark eyes glinting malevolently. His breathing changed and he closed the gap between them, his breathing altering. Her pulse slammed at the base of her throat, and she retreated as he matched her step for step until she was pressed against the wall.

"Where are you going, Mary?"

"I have work to do," she blurted out, her bravado scattering under his predatory look.

"You're really very pretty, Mary. I could make you a happy woman, you know…"

"For God's sake, Peter," the duke's bored voice boomed from the doorway, "stop bothering the help."

Peter stilled; the ardent light extinguished from his eyes as he stepped back with a frustrated sigh. "Father… I'm not bothering anyone, am I, Mary?"

Trixie slid along the wall towards her escape, not bothering to answer him. The duke poured himself a drink from the decanter, staring at her and then his son. She grabbed up her bucket and brush with a hurried apology and fled the room as the voices between father and son escalated into one of their regular arguments. She walked part-way along the hall and had to lower the bucket of water before she dropped it. She pressed her fingers to her lips, the tears burning the back of her eyes as she started to shake. She gulped in air to steady herself as footsteps echoed up the stairs, knuckling at the tears that spilled over her lids. Regardless of what Anna and Stella wanted, she needed to get out of here – the sooner, the better. The duke might not be around next time.

❧

"So, this is where you've been hiding?"

Trixie jolted at the slurred words and spun to face Peter, clutching at her chest. She'd been absorbed in attending to the lamps, lighting them in each of the rooms that guests may want to use. She was following the house-keeper's instructions to remain as invisible as possible. The laughter and the chatter from the party guests were at all an all-time high as Trixie had slipped in and out of the rooms. 'All hands on deck' Mrs Martin had called tonight, as she'd barked out instructions to each member of staff that morning in the kitchen.

"Peter," she breathed, "you scared me!"

He rolled around the door frame, wagging a long finger at her. "That isn't how you should address me, and you know it. Now, come here so that I can chastise you appropriately,"

Trixie's eyes slid to the closed door. *No escape.* Even if she yelled, no one would hear her above the din of his party. No one would care for a scrap of a servant being mauled by someone of standing. "Pardon me, Your Grace – shouldn't you be attending your party guests?"

He weaved unsteadily on his feet. Even in the muted light, she could see the fierce mania burning in his eyes. Her pulse kicked up at the agitation that seemed to roll from him as he walked towards her. "I only have eyes for you, my little wench. Come here to me,"

She dodged around his outstretched hand and ran for the door, unable to mute the scream that was torn from her throat as he grabbed her cap and a fistful of her hair. "No!"

He wrapped his arms around her, fetid breath brushing across her ear as his hands closed over her breasts. "Mmm, that's better. Keep wriggling, it helps,"

She dug her nails into the back of his hands and threw back her head, connecting with a satisfying thud that had him howling. Without looking back, she bolted for the door. She was halfway along the hall when she saw him lumbering after her. She turned for the stairs, her young legs out-pumping his inebriated ones and she rounded the landing. *Down,* she chastised herself. She should have gone down where she might have been in the safety of other staff. Up here, it was empty. She tried doors, rattling the handles in futility. Each one was locked. Mrs Martin and her blasted obsession with security.

Peter rounded the top of the stairs, his singsong voice taunting her. Trixie sprinted further into the belly of the house, trying to get a head start on him. Door after door, until finally, one sprung open and she fell through it, closing it softly so as not to give him any clue that she'd found a hiding place. The room was almost pitch black and she had to wait for her eyes to adjust for a moment. She could just about make out the grand four-poster bed, and shadowy hulks of the armoire and drawers, a desk, heavy curtains parted back from the wide windows with the lacy thin covering fluttering in the cool night air where the window had been left slightly open. She heard Peter outside, calling her name, and quickly, she ducked under the bed, trying to hold onto her ragged gasps. Her heart roared in her ears, even as she heard him staggering past the room.

She waited for a few more minutes, the silence ringing, then she wriggled back out from under the bed, blowing out a breath. She took the matches in her apron pocket and lit the lamp that sat on the rosewood chiffonier, hoping to find a looking glass to be able to straighten her hair where he'd pulled it. The last thing she needed to do was to have to explain away her state of dishevelment to someone else. The soft lamp glow spread around the room as she looked about. Slowly, a smile crossed her lips. The furnishings were grand in here, grander than in most rooms. Floral patterned walls from skirting to coving, matching furniture with ornate inlays and more pillows on the bed than you could shake a stick at.

The duke's bedroom. Someone must have forgotten to lock the door, with everything going on tonight. Trixie crossed to the bureau, nudging back the heavy chair and she tried the drawer. Locked. She rifled through the contents of the desk, snatching at the letter opener before she jammed it into the lock, wiggling the blade until finally, there was a click. She pulled on the drawer. Reaching for the lamp so that she could see better, she pawed through the contents, picking up and discarding the pieces of paper in there when none of them displayed the insignia that she'd been told to look for. She nearly let out a bellow of frustration. It was all just banal chitchat, arranging family gatherings, planning meetings, and social events. Nothing like she'd been told to look for.

She sat back on her heels, blinking at her tears. *I can't do it.* She sniffed, wiping at her eyes. It was useless. She was useless. She plopped down on the floor, staring miserably at the desk when something caught her eye. She grabbed the lamp and held it into the space under the desk. There, at the back of the desk, was what looked like a small knot of wood. A knot with the gold glint of brass in the centre. She pressed the knot and it pushed in, then popped back out with a resounding click. And there, hidden in the recess of the duke's desk, was a bundle of letters, each with the double-headed eagle of the Russian Empire on.

CHAPTER 8

❧

$\mathcal{T}$rixie

"COME ON!" Anna ordered her reproachfully, "Hurry up!"

Trixie jogged behind her, reminded of the night that they'd fled the duke's property only last month. Just like that night, moonlight illuminated their path along the road that they'd hurried down and they'd lurked in bushes until a carriage had met them at a rendezvous point in the early morning mists. Unlike that night, Trixie had been happy to get out of there.

"Why are we running? I hadn't even started the job, let alone had the chance to finish it." She'd been getting ready for bed when Anna had barged into the room that she shared with two other maids and asked to speak to her. Anna had made her leave all her possessions behind, including her little case that had followed her everywhere since she'd left London.

"Because, Miss Idiot, the duke made a drawing of me, worked with one of the police artists. My picture is all over the front of newspapers and things. Now everyone is looking for me on account of his jewels being stolen," She swung back round to meet Trixie, jabbed an accusing finger at her and Trixie halted before she collided with the digit. "You were only meant to take the letters, nowt else! And don't give me no cock an' bull story about him saying it's diamonds just to make a criminal case. I know you took other things. I just know it!"

"I'll tell you again for the hundredth time – I only took the letters. He can't very well go to the police and ask for them back – he was blackmailing people!"

"You're a snivelling foozler, Mary!"

Trixie planted her hands on her hips. "Where are they then? These jewels? I've been stuck with you the whole time. From when we left the old place, to when we spent the night at that hotel, to when we arrived here. Where have I been to be able to sell the stuff?"

"You could have hidden them!"

"Didn't I follow you straight out of the house tonight?" She spread her hands in a show of innocence, widening her eyes slightly. "If I had stolen anything, wouldn't I have had to go back to my room for it?"

"You're a thief – and a good one," Anna informed her darkly. "You could have easily dumped them somewhere and gone back for them later. You could…"

"I can hear you from the other street," a male voice

muttered, making Anna yelp and Trixie jump. "You might want to tone it down and shift your backside, seeing as you're a wanted criminal."

Trixie stared at the form, familiarity tickling her memory. And without hesitation, she ran at full tilt into George's open arms.

～

"WHERE IS SHE GOING?" Trixie watched as the battered-looking wagon trundled and was swallowed by the darkness.

George settled himself on the bench opposite her and tapped twice on the cab wall. The hansom carriage jerked as it was set into motion. George smirked, "Do you care? Sounded like the two of you weren't getting along,"

Trixie lifted a shoulder and turned to look out into the crisp air. The road was darker now that they'd moved beyond the town limits. "She was the worst one I've ever worked with,"

"Did you take any diamonds?"

Trixie turned her head back to him, putting an appropriate level of offence into her face, even as she could feel the gems rubbing where she'd stitched them into her vest. The black pouch full of diamonds had been in front of the letters she'd found. And she could see how she might escape the clutches of Stella – so, she'd taken them. "Of course not,"

"You've gotten better at lying," he said, mouth twisting sardonically. He leaned forward, resting his forearms on his knees. "Just make sure you get rid of them soon. Do it away from any cities. Find a pawn shop in a smaller town. I could do it if you like,"

She blinked, wondering how he could tell, what her tells were – and how she could improve them. "I didn't take them."

George held her gaze momentarily then he reached across and ruffled her hair. "You've gotten taller,"

She didn't allow her relief to show. She hated lying to her only friend, but he seemed content to spend his days beating and taking in the name of Stella. "You haven't."

He huffed out a laugh and sat back.

"Am I going back to London?" she asked when he continued to stare at her.

"Would you like to?"

"I'd like to see Lily," she said, her voice thick with the emotion that she tried to keep contained. "I miss her,"

"Lily is doing just fine, Trix," he replied gently. "She shows me your letters – she is proud that you're doing so well. She brags to the others that she's your sister,"

A tear splashed on her cheek as her eyes drifted closed. "Proud of a thief? Hardly something to be delighted with."

George dragged off his billy cap and he sat forward again, threaded it through his fingers as it dangled between his open knees. "Stella... she keeps her protected. Away from the business. Lily doesn't know what it is that you do – she thinks that you're a maid, or whatever they have you doing at the time you write to her. She doesn't associate with the other girls, has no idea how Stella feeds all those children. It's almost like... as if Stella is her mother and Lily, is her daughter. She's like Stella's protégé."

Trixie frowned; her throat constricted as conflicting emotions rippled through her. Lily was cocooned... secure. Wasn't that the agreement that she'd struck with the crime boss? And yet, Trixie had had to ensure much to facilitate that protection... A wave of jealousy flooded her, and she cast her eyes down, ashamed. Lily was safe and that's all that should matter.

"What's that look for?" he reproached gently.

Trixie shook her head, setting her shoulders back as she met his concerned look. "Nothing," she peeled back her lips, mask firmly back in place. "Anna said that we were pulled from the house because her photo is being circulated. Is there one of me, too?"

Affection flickered in his eyes. "No, just hers. The duke is making lots of noise about the alleged theft of the diamonds – no mention of the letters, of course. He believes you to be her daughter and that she committed the crime. Seems the duke thinks a thirteen-year-old couldn't pull off that kind of stunt under his nose."

Her face crinkled in concern. "Does Stella think I took diamonds, too?"

"No. If she does, she hasn't shared that with me."

Trixie digested that as she watched the scene beyond the glass roll past. She hadn't known why she took the stones. She certainly wouldn't be able to get rid of them just yet, but the opportunity had presented itself, and she'd acted upon it. She'd known that it was wrong –

though wasn't she a thief? Why wouldn't she become a swindler, too?

"Where am I going, then? Another house? Shoplifting?"

"You're too good for hoisting, now." George sank back against the upholstered bench, fidgeted to get more comfortable. "You need to lie low for a while until this hullabaloo blows over, and it seems that Stella has bigger plans for her best girl, Trixie-Lix. You've put the duke in Stella's pocket – that means you've been promoted once more."

"Why were you sent to meet me? I know it's not because you missed me."

His lips twitched as he closed his eyes. "You're going for more training. I'm taking you to meet a cracksman."

She frowned at him. "A safe cracker? Why?"

George settled his billy cap on his face and exhaled tiredly. "Always with the questions."

As George's snores filled the cab and the dawn began to edge back the darkness across the world beyond the glass her breath frosted against, Trixie wondered what turn her life would take next.

~

FELIX

WITH HIS BREATH pluming in front of his face, Felix took a handful of the cold, damp soil and sprinkled it onto the top of the plain wooden coffin, the same as he'd watched the other mourners do.

He was surrounded in a sea of black clothing, the fog cloaking them all where they stood in the graveyard so that the yew trees appeared murky in the gloomy morning light. His father had been buried in the spring – a funeral in the winter seemed more apt to him.

Mrs Akerman's gloved hand took him by the wrist, moving with the rest of the parish who'd turned out to pay their respects to Father Frank Huxley. "Come, Felix, we must go and meet Florence – she'll be waiting for us,"

At the mention of her daughter's name, Felix felt himself resisting the old housekeeper's guiding hand. She had arrived the day after Frank had died and seemed intent on plundering the house of furniture. He'd found her burning his beloved books and had slapped him back when he'd tried to stop her.

"No dilly-dallying, child, she'll only get cross and I'm in no mood to deal with her today."

"Shouldn't we go with the rest of the congregation?" Felix asked, his eyes drifting to where the flow of people was moving away from him, back towards the refectory.

For a moment, he wondered if she'd heard him and he looked at her, about to repeat himself, when she sent him a sheepish look. "No time… Come on, Felix, walk faster."

The sinking sensation of grief that had filled him since the morning he'd found Frank still in his bed now moved to one of dread and foreboding. "Where are we going? Mrs Akerman? What's going on?"

Mrs Akerman pursed her lips, ignoring his querulous

tone, and pulled him towards the end of the lane where he could see a black hansom waiting. The curtain moved and the door opened as they approached, where Florence reclined on one of the seats.

"Up you go," Mrs Akerman said quickly, "come on now, Felix."

His eyes darted behind the old woman, searching for rescue, but the lane was now empty. "I…"

"Get in here, you brat," Florence screeched, "I haven't got all day!"

Felix scrambled up, sitting as far away from Florence as he could, avoiding the baleful looks she was giving him. He wanted to ask where he was going but didn't like the fast hands that the housekeeper's daughter used on him.

"What took you so long?" Florence demanded of her mother, "It's too cold to be sat about waiting on you,"

"Sorry, Florence, but I can't make the ceremony go any faster. I'm sure people were already talking about me. This doesn't feel right. And Felix… he's just a boy."

"Well, no one asked you how you feel," Florence said abrasively. "I told you we didn't have long before the officials will come and take that house back. You earned what we've taken, Ma. They wouldn't have let you have what was rightfully yours. You would have been thrown out on your ear with no reference because he died!"

"Maybe the bishop would have…"

"You're too foolish to realise that they would throw you out. Who would employ someone as old as you, Mother? You can barely stay upright these days. No, this was the best course of action to take – and you're lucky I was here to help you."

Felix watched the old housekeeper, her usual brisk and efficient manner now eclipsed by this obedient and scared woman, who dabbed the end of her pointy nose.

"What if they come looking for me, Florence?"

"All the reason to dump the boy and get gone! I let you stay for the funeral for that stupid old man,"

"He wasn't stupid," Felix stated under his breath and was rewarded with a stinging slap for his effort.

"You shut your mouth – you'll soon learn your place and to keep it buttoned," Florence said snidely.

Felix bit the inside of his cheek to stop himself from crying. Florence had dominated the past two weeks, demanding, and snarling at anyone who she came across. In part, he was happy that they were leaving him behind. He looked out of the window, recognising the small road that the carriage was moving along, and his fear came alive in his veins. He could see the short, stumpy chimneys that poked up from the long, narrow roof above the treeline and, as they turned into the wide driveway, rows of tall rectangular windows in the red-bricked edifice came into view. *The workhouse.* He sent a look of terror at Mrs Akerman who turned away from him, shame-faced.

The carriage drew to a stop, and a young boy opened the door, his pock-marked complexion ruddy from the cold morning air. An older, well-dressed man appeared behind him, giving the group a smile that didn't quite reach his eyes. Felix took one look at him and slid away from the opening until he bumped into Mrs Akerman.

"Morning, ladies. Hello, Felix, I'm Mr Thomas, master of the workhouse. Pleased to meet you,"

"Come now, *Felix*," Florence said, the vice-like grip that bruised his arm was in direct contrast to her pleasant tone, "there's nothing to worry about,"

"That's right, young man. Let's not keep these fine ladies hanging around on such a cold day – it isn't polite." He took a hold of Felix's other arm and the boy fell down the steps, saved from hitting the ground by the man's grasp. "We'll look after you here at…". Florence had pulled the door shut, cutting off the man's words and she banged twice on the interior of the cab. The carriage lurched forward, and Felix yelled at them to stop, not to leave him, stretching impotently at the retreat.

Mr Thomas yanked him back. "We'll have none of that misbehaviour. Inside, now – let's get you settled in."

"No!" Felix resisted, digging his heels into the stoned driveway. "Wait!"

"William, come and help me here, will you?" Mr Thomas summoned the boy who'd opened the door.

"Yes, Master Thomas,"

Felix was lifted into the air, suspended by his limbs as he was carried through the front door of the workhouse.

CHAPTER 9

*T*rixie

"I DON'T THINK I could ever tire of this view," Morgan exclaimed as he stopped near the gate. With his foot on the bottom rung of the gate and his arms resting on the top, his clear blue gaze drifted out across the rolling hills, the patchwork greens and yellows of the fields basking in the pleasant May sunshine.

Trixie wasn't taken in by the view though; she couldn't tear her eyes from him. She examined the planes of his face, the long lashes bleached blond at the tips, how the dimple flashed in his cheek when he turned to her and smiled.

"What are you staring at?"

She checked that the rest of the staff were out of sight before she stepped to him and bumped him with her shoulder. They were all making the walk back from the Sunday sermon. "You," she said, playfully. He checked that the quiet lane was empty before he turned to her fully and dipped his head to hers for a kiss. He turned her blood thick and gloopy like molasses, and she rolled her lips inwards when he straightened as if to hold onto the lingering touch.

"I'm sure we shouldn't be canoodling out in the open," he admonished softly in his delightful Welsh brogue, "but you turn my head. You have since the very first moment you arrived at the manor house."

She sighed, basking in the happiness that filled her up as she leaned her head on his shoulder to gaze out across the countryside that he was admiring moments before. He swung his arm up around her shoulder and pressed a kiss to her head. "I could stay this way forever," she murmured.

"Sunday's do seem to go by so fast. Do you think you could maybe swing your next afternoon off on Wednesday? Mr Doyle says I can take that day off. Thought we might go for a walk to the farm, see my father and my mother."

Trixie turned her head to look up at him, her gaze searching his as a frisson of excitement burst inside. She knew that he had humble beginnings – as a footman to the manor house, he'd started mucking out the stables to earn a coin and had worked hard to get to the position of a footman. But she had never met his family. "Have you told them about me?"

His gaze sobered as he looked down into her hopeful

face. "Would you mind if I had? I know you're a secretive sort, Mary Jones,"

She lowered her gaze as guilt bloomed in her stomach. She had never planned on falling in love with Morgan Ellis. She had arrived at the house last winter, fresh after the training from George and the strange cracksman. The manor was at the edges of a tiny village, far from the city, from newspapers and the prying eyes of the peerage.

She had been told she was to hide away here until everything had died down. That's what she did. For months, she had worked hard as a chambermaid, kept her head down and her mouth shut, waiting on instructions from Stella. As spring thawed out the wintry months, she'd begun to settle into the rural life.

At first, her prickly nature had kept the charming Morgan at bay. She didn't put down any roots. She was meant to do the job and move on; that had been her life for years. No point in making friends, and it was too dangerous to reveal anything about herself. But the staff at the manor house made it hard not to start to relax. They were a cheerful bunch, motivated by a good employer and proud of the fact that they worked at such a prestigious property. The days grew longer, and Trixie relaxed more. Encouraged by the housekeeper, Mrs Baxter, and the ever-romantic Belle, Trixie had begun to see the footman in a different light.

As she had warmed up to the prospect of staying in a job, she had started to dream of having a normal life. One of having a home that she could call her own... a husband... children. Having the chance of a normal life.

Now, she lived with the dread that this would all end, that she would be pulled away from here, back to her old life.

He lifted her chin with a crooked finger. "What is it, Mary? What did I say to put the shadows in your eyes?"

She shook her head and bit the inside of her lip to stop her from blurting out the truth. Her name wasn't Mary, it was Trixie. She wasn't a maid, but she was a thief, in hiding. Could she trust him? "I'll see if I can work my charm on Mrs Baxter. If not, I'll try Mr. Doyle."

Morgan chuckled and gave her shoulder an encouraging squeeze. "I'm sure as eggs is eggs that you'll get your own way. Nobody seems to be able to say 'no' to you,"

Her laugh was husky and she had to move away from him. Being this close to him was making her soft. "You flatter me, Morgan," She caught the flicker of confusion that pulled on his brows, and she smiled. "I shall be delighted to meet your family, though I'm not sure how they'll feel meeting a maid for their son, especially one that isn't chaperoned. It isn't really proper now, is it?"

Morgan tipped his head as he considered. "Well, certainly, I'd like to meet your father one day. And pay my respects to your Ma's grave,"

She nodded with her head, uncomfortable when the subject shone on the lies that she'd spun on her arrival. It was her usual back story – her father worked hard, couldn't afford to feed his children after her mother had passed on. "We should get back, the other's will be wondering where we've got to,"

He fell into step beside her. "I'm sure they'll draw their

own conclusions and tease us both about them at supper time."

"That they will," They stepped onto the grass verge as a hansom cab careened past them, horses white with sweat.

"What idiots are going that fast," Morgan cursed, viciously. "I'm guessing that they're not locals – I didn't recognise them,"

Trixie dismissed the cab with a shrug as they continued along the road. "They were going too fast for me to see. How far is it to your family farm?"

"Not far," Morgan explained, "I might see if I can use one of the wagons. I'll explain that I could pick up some supplies up in the town, that may swing it,"

"Will they let you use it?" Trixie asked in surprise.

Morgan slid her a conspiratorial wink. "Probably not, but I know someone who could persuade Mrs Baxter that we need it."

Trixie rolled her eyes playfully as she stepped through the gate that he held for her and they started up the long winding drive towards the manor house. "You set an awful lot of faith in me."

Morgan caught her hand and brought it to his lips. "I'll always believe in you, Mary. You're my girl."

Trixie stilled, heart fluttering wildly as she stared at him. "What did you say?"

He tugged on her hand, pulling her closer to him. The wind ruffled his blond hair and the dimple flashed in the sunlight. His arms slid around her waist, and she tried to resist, knowing that they were in view of the house where they stood. "I don't care that people can see," he said laughingly. "What does it matter anyway? I'm taking you to my parents to announce that I'm planning on asking you to marry me. It was meant to be a surprise, but I can't keep it in." The shock made her body lax, and she sank against him. "I love you, Mary," he purred, "More than I could ever love anything. Will you be mine?"

Even as the carriage careened back past behind them, the shouts of jeering from the driver were lost in the fog of enthralment that he held over her. She loved him, right on back, though her throat ached, and she could only mutely nod through the tears. He held her, spun her in a circle, and whooped his joy.

"Let's keep it to ourselves, now, okay?" he lowered her back down, blue eyes looking to the house, "that's if no one has seen us here, though I'm as happy as a lark on the first day of spring right now, and that's the truth."

"Me, too," she croaked, "Me, too, Morgan."

"Oh, come on, now," he passed her his handkerchief, "no tears. No girl of mine will cry. What will Mrs Baxter say if she sees you've been crying?"

A brief laugh broke from her. "She'll never let up until I tell her."

She followed him up the rest of the drive, allowing the memory of his words to wash over her. *My girl.* It warmed her, from deep within. Finally, she felt like she belonged to someone. That she would have someone on her side.

"Ready?" he asked, shooting her a grin.

She nodded and gave him his handkerchief back. "How do I look?"

"Like the most beautiful girl on God's green earth," he winked.

"Get on with you," she pushed him away laughing. The smile played around her mouth as they entered through the servant's entrance, hanging their coats up in the cloakroom.

"Oh, there you both are," Mr Doyle, the butler, waved them through into the open kitchen space. "What took you? Come, come. We have news."

Trixie drew up short when she rounded the corner, her stomach doing a long slow roll as she met the familiar face of Mildred, one of Stella's girls from her first-ever job. The dread that had been lingering on the periphery of her life, lurking menacingly, now blasted through her. All attention was on the new girl so only Mildred caught the frozen expression on Trixie's face as introductions were made. She replied mechanically, pretending like they hadn't known each other previously. That was the code.

Mildred could only be here for one thing, and one thing only. Trixie the thief was back in business.

≈

"You have yourself a nice little comfortable job here, don't you, *Mary*?"

Trixie's hand stilled at the drawled tone from behind her. It was as if her mind had conjured up the other woman – she'd thought of nothing since she'd hastily made her escape and gone to bed early last night. Even as Belle had retired and crept about the room, Trixie had feigned sleep. Misery cloaked her. She had to keep control of herself and her emotions.

"I'd hardly call scrubbing bare floors comfortable," she focused on emptying the bucket in the sink and dried it carefully. "What's the job?" She heard the door click closed and when she turned, Mildred was leaning back against it, her eyes glittered dangerously.

"Are you quite mad? Someone could hear you!"

Trixie lifted a brow. "Even if they did, they wouldn't get my meaning. They're an open and happy bunch – they don't see shadows and bandits straightaway,"

Mildred folded her arms, her nostrils pinched white in disapproval. "Has Stella's best girl turned soft?"

Trixie mimicked the other woman's stance, leaning back against the deep sink. "I'm bored, Mildred. Stuck in the back end of nowhere with nothing to do. I thought I'd been forgotten about,"

Mildred curled her lip derisively. "'hoped' might be a better description, going by the look on your face yesterday when I arrived. Besides, I saw you snuggled up to your country bumpkin when I passed on by you yesterday – is that how you've been earning your coin? On your back for the locals?" She elbowed off the door and sauntered towards Trixie, malevolence twinkling in her dark eyes. "Or are you giving it to him for free, thinking that you can stay here in obscurity?"

"What is the job?" Trixie deadpanned, keeping her face carefully blank. Mildred's words, designed to get a reaction, struck home painfully. Morgan and his kind face swam in her mind's eye, and she longed to scratch the spitefulness out of Mildred's face.

Mildred sniggered. "You're to grab what you can from here. We are to meet a pickup on Thursday night."

Guilt from this collusion rolled in her stomach but she kept her gaze level. Her employers were good people; they'd been kind to a fault and were nice to their staff. They didn't deserve to have that trust broken. "You're giving me three days? They have nothing. The family isn't a wealthy one, there isn't a big haul to take. I'm a criminal, not a magician,"

"You've had nigh on six months to case this joint – make it work. It's time to up and leave."

"I've already checked what they have," Trixie lied. "They have nothing."

"They can't have a house the size of this and not have a few trinkets worth a bob or two worth nicking,"

"Why are you here then? If you're only here for a few days."

"Probably to keep an eye on you. Stella must have known that you'd turn soft on her. Wait 'til she finds out you're smooching with the locals,"

Trixie wondered what she must have seen as the carriage had raced past her and Morgan, though she could only recall the bubble of joy that she'd been cocooned in. "I wasn't smooching with him and…" She bit back the words that wanted to tumble out.

"And what?" Speculation twisted Mildred's thin lips. "Is the thief girl in love?"

Trixie turned back to the sink, injecting boredom into

her tone. "I'll have the job done by Thursday night. Be ready to leave by the time the clock strikes twelve,"

Trixie held her breath as she heard the click of Mildred's shoes get closer. "We leave at eleven," she whispered in a lethal tone. "This place has made you forget your place, girl."

As Mildred firmly shut the door behind her, Trixie let her breath out and her tears fell unchecked down her cheeks. At that moment, she would have given anything to disappear. To grab Morgan and for them to vanish, far away where Stella wouldn't find them. Hadn't George said that Lily was safe – Stella's protégé. Did that mean that Stella had come to care for the young girl? Surely, Lily would be okay now if Trixie chose to flee. Even if she were to go back, her life was so different from Lily's. Would they have anything in common again? For the first time, she finally understood why Angela had run. She had fallen in love with the man who'd been shouting in the street that day,

Maybe on Wednesday when they had the wagon, she could persuade Morgan to keep going. Angela had disappeared – she'd managed to escape the clutches of the queen of thieves. Trixie could do the same.

~

FELIX

. . .

MOONLIGHT SLANTED through the small round window, high up in the wall, its eerie light cutting across the dormitory floor. Identical beds filled the space, lined up with military precision. Each bed had a thin, itchy blanket. Felix wondered idly if the scrawny children who now filled the beds shivered under them as much as he now was on their first night in the workhouse. He lay on his back as it seemed to ease his back where he'd been struck. He was watching the black circle and tried to picture which stars he'd be able to see. He closed his eyes, desperately trying to recall what Andrew had called it… *astronomy*. The study of the sky, and beyond. A heartfelt smile touched his lips as he remembered their visit to one of the many institutions. Frank discreetly sipped from his whisky flask as he'd followed Andrew and Felix, feigning disinterest yet asking pertinent questions that made Andrew wink at Felix. Andrew had described a machine that was powerful enough to be able to see these stars up close.

His hand went to his throat, a practised action since Andrew had left over a year ago, but it was now bare. His beloved ankh, torn off his neck and then thrown on the fire by the plump matron.

"We'll have no such wickedness in this place! I cannot believe Father Frank would allow such pagan attributes in his presence. You must have the devil in you, boy!"

When he'd fought to get his gift back, the matron had claimed it illustrated her point and he'd needed to have the devil beaten out of him. With each strike against his back, Felix had called for help, for someone to save him.

Two hands pinning his arms on either side of him inside the blanket made his eyes fly open. In the ghostly light, William's pockmarked face looked even more grisly, his dark eyes lit maniacally.

"Look who it is, boys!" Spittle dripped from his mouth onto Felix's face. "It's the devil worshipper!"

Felix's eyes whirled and he sucked in a breath to scream for help, but a beefy hand clapped it shut again. He fought against the confines of the restraining weight atop of him and waited for the pain to start.

CHAPTER 10

❧

𝒯rixie

"YOU DON'T SEEM YOURSELF, MARY," Morgan commented, his eyes fixed ahead.

Trixie blinked, bringing herself back to the moment. "Pardon?"

"My point exactly," he said with a wry smile. "You have been distracted since I told you that I loved you. I thought that maybe you'd changed your mind on agreeing to marry a man such as myself, but then you agreed to come with me today. Though, you seem to want to be anywhere else but here with me. It isn't much further to go. I know it's only a humble farm – I would work hard to provide for you, and any children that we may be blessed with."

Her cheeks grew pink. She could see now how it must look to him. She placed a hand on his forearm, and he turned to look at the touch, then met her gaze. "I have been distracted, but not because I changed my mind," her heart quickened, and her mouth was suddenly dry.

How was she to start? She desperately wanted him to understand, to come away with her. The thought of not seeing him every day was splitting her in half. Mildred had hounded her for the past two days, laying on the pressure for her to break the safe in the old man's office. She had resisted the urge to yell and scream at the other maid, sticking to the plan that had begun forming in her mind at the sink the other day. The more that she thought about it, the more it had seemed to be her only opportunity to escape. "You're a good man, Morgan Ellis, and any woman worth her salt would be lucky to have a man like yourself to call their own."

His sharp blue eyes swung to meet hers, his gaze searching. He turned the horse and wagon to the side of the road and turned to face her on the bench that they shared. "That sentence sounds like there is a 'but' in there somewhere, Mary."

Her tongue shot out to moisten her lips and she touched her bonnet self-consciously. "I don't..." She cleared her throat, trying to hold back the tide of tears and emotions that boiled inside her. "I do love you, Morgan, but there are some things that you should know about me. Things that may make you change your mind." She lost the battle and tears filled her eyes.

Morgan took her hands in his, his thumbs caressing the backs of her hands. "Mary, please, you're killing me here. What is it that hurts you so?"

She dragged her eyes up to meet him, as the truth pressed against her conscience. She'd had to hide who she was for so long, it felt strange to admit her true feelings out loud. "My name isn't Mary," she whispered thickly, "It's Trixie."

He blinked, and his brow furrowed as he waited for more from her, but she held back, gauging his response. "Is that it? Your big secret is that you changed your name? Did you not like your given name?"

His unashamed innocence made her smile, gave her hope. "Not quite,"

"Then why, Mar – I mean, Trixie. Whatever it is, we can get through this. I love you, and I want to spend my days with you."

Buoyed by his optimistic words and the longing for the notion of a life with him, she exhaled. "Do you truly mean that? Because I want that, too."

"Yes, I do," he squeezed her hands, giving her encouragement. "Tell me what's going on."

"I want you to run away with me,"

He laughed softly. "Run away? Where would we go?"

"I don't care," Trixie shook her head. "Anywhere you want to – far away from here, from England,"

"Why? Why would I leave my good job? I hope to be butler one day – we can live a comfortable life in the village – or any village, if you like," He shook his head as he considered her. "But I don't want to leave my family, my home. This is all I've known all my life."

Trixie slumped in her seat, her mind sifting through ways to persuade him to change his mind. "It wouldn't matter where we live. I could pay for lodgings; we could get jobs somewhere else. Please, Morgan, oh, say you will."

"You're not making any sense, Mary, or Trixie. Whoever you are. How would you afford for us to live anywhere? Are you a secret heiress?"

She shook her head despondently.

"What then? What are you running from?"

"My old life," she replied dully. "My old boss. I'm a thief, Morgan. I was sent here to hide out. My boss has sent for me…"

He dropped her hands, physically shifted back in his seat as he stared at her. Right then, pain shafted through her, and she felt the chasm of loss erupt between them as he withdrew. She'd never felt such an acute critical analysis of her being as she did now. "You're a *thief*? Mary… Trixie… you steal things? You were sent here to *steal*?"

She closed her eyes to his judgement and her tears seeped through her lashes as she nodded.

"Why would you do such a thing? I thought you were a good Christian… I…" The wagon shifted as he altered his position and when she looked upon him again, he was facing forward, his elbows on his knees. "You lied to me, to everyone." He looked back at her, accusingly. "You led me a merry dance and made me look a fool. How am I meant to trust you, woman? I can't even bring myself to say your name!" His brogue grew harsh, and his face twisted in anger. He yanked his arm out of her way as she reached for him.

"Morgan, please, I beg you…"

"No!" he roared. "I don't want you near me."

"I'm sorry, just let me explain…"

"You can't truly know me to think that I would live my life with a dirty thief. And I suppose you were going to pay for our lodgings with what you stole from honest, hardworking people, taking from them? You disgust me," he hissed, fury dripping from his voice.

She covered her face, shame burning through her.

"I don't care for your tears. You don't even deserve my pity. And you can walk back to the manor house – I will not discredit my family's name by allowing someone of your low morals to cross their threshold."

She lowered her hands, looking at him but he was closed off, staring ahead stonily. "You want me to go?"

"Get away from me. I don't care where you go, I just don't want to see your deceitful face ever again." He snapped.

Trixie took the basket that she'd set behind her, dismissing the memories where she'd carefully packed it with tasty morsels for them to enjoy from the pantry, pushing away the dreams where he'd accepted who she truly was and had thanked her for thinking to bring food and refreshments as they'd disappeared. In the bottom, she'd hidden her small reticule and the diamonds. She clambered down from the wagon, leaping back as he'd slapped the reins against the horse's back and the wagon jolted forwards. Trixie stood in the middle of the road, watching as the trail of dust that kicked up from the wagon dissipated in the warm spring breeze, just like the hopes and dreams she'd held for a happy future with Morgan.

≈

FELIX

"FELIX BAKER!"

Felix wanted to duck his head into his shoulders as the matron's voice cut across the kitchen space, but he knew that having his back to her was usually seen as an invitation to strike him. He turned towards her, kept his head bowed as she liked, "Yes, Miss McDonald?"

"The master wants to see you, right away. Stop what you're doing and go there now."

Felix dropped the potato into the sink full of peelings and stepped down from the upturned bucket. Several sets of eyes tracked his progress across the quarry-tiled floor, and he saw William draw a finger across his throat in warning. Felix knew what happened to boys who tattled on the older children, and he knew to keep his mouth shut. Matron gave him a shove through the door to help him on his way and he trotted ahead of her, to stay out of the range of her ham-sized fists. A frisson of cold dread licked along his blood when he could hear raised voices echoing along the hallway, especially when he realised that it was emanating from the master's office. He must have slowed his pace as Matron's hand was on his back, propelling him through the door without warning.

"Ah, there he is, young Felix Baker!" Master Thomas rose from behind his desk, eyes bright though his face was beet-red.

But it was the other man who was stood in the space that drew Felix's attention. "Andrew?"

Sporting the same scruffy beard and long mane of hair that he'd had the first time Felix had seen him, Andrew's teeth appeared in the centre of the fur. "Hello, my dear Felix."

For a moment, Felix wondered if he was still asleep, as he'd dreamed of this moment many times in the past nine months. He stared at the apparition and waited for the morning gong to wake him. But there was no bell, no alarm. Andrew's warm gaze flickered as they scanned the small boy, with his eye swollen shut and bruised to black. Instead of rebuking him, or a harsh word, he simply opened his arms and caught the skinny boy in a hug.

~

TRIXIE

THE BITTER WIND blasted down the street and Trixie hunched her shoulders, tucking her hands into her shawl in a bid to stave off the chill. She followed the main flow of people, watching their movements.

Winter was always hard though she would swear under oath that the wind in the north was harsher than any in London. It also meant heavy winter coats over the top of valuables, and they were less likely to be lifted. She crossed the street, leaping over puddles that gathered in the street corner and lumps that didn't move in the road, determined in her steps as she tracked a plump woman resplendent in feathers and finery, walking with purpose towards the town centre. Still, when she brushed past the woman as she deliberately intersected her trajectory, it was easy enough to lift her purse from her pocket, especially as the daft woman had allowed the drawstrings to dangle from the opening. Anyone foolish enough to be out in this weather was easy pickings.

Trixie made her way back towards the lodgings, pleased that she would be out of this inclement weather sooner now that she didn't have to make a trip to the pawnshop first. She bounced the bag of coins lightly in her palm as she thought about the hot bowl of stew and an extra slice of fluffy bread and a thick layer of salty butter on top of it. She opened the door to the hotel, almost sighed her relief from the heat of the log fire that simmered in the hearth.

"Alright, Miss Winters? Manage to find any work today?"

Trixie cupped her hands around her lips and blew into the hole as she hurried to the fire and held out her hands. "Yes, I did, thank you."

The old woman stared at her. "At the cotton factory? They taking on again?"

Trixie snorted. "Not a sniff, am afraid, Agnes. All locked up, I suppose until this freeze eases off. I was down where the barges are, asked a man there if he needed help unloading some things. He didn't want to but agreed that he'd be out of this cold snap sooner if I helped."

"Aye, sounds about right," the woman shook her head. "Sad to see so many people wandering the streets, them with little 'uns to feed, too. You'll be staying another night?"

"Yes, for now. And I'll take a bowl if you've cooked, I don't happen to care what as everything you make is delicious."

Agnes preened under the compliment and she hurried off towards the kitchen. By the time Trixie let herself into the room, she was suitably satiated and could feel lethargy stealing up her legs. She shut the door behind her, but it was the scraping of a shoe along the bare floorboards that had her spinning around, the scream trapped in her throat.

"Finally," the voice husked, and sent a tremor of fear shooting down her spine. Trixie held the lamp aloft to see better through the gloom. "You took your time." The hawk-eyed stare of Stella watched her carefully.

∽

FELIX

"MY BROTHER HAD PROPERTY, an estate – what happened to it?" Andrew straightened up but kept a large hand on Felix's shoulder.

Mr Thomas mimicked the action though it took him a

moment to stand up. "I'm afraid I'm not privy to that information, Mr Huxley. Master Baker arrived with no property, other than the clothes he stood in. We've fed and kept him in good health for the past nine months, as you can see."

"I suppose you're not privy to how my young charge got the black eye, either?" Andrew's calm tone sounded lethal. "Also, my brother had Felix's name changed legally to Felix Huxley, Mr. Thomas – and I'll thank you to respect that."

The fury that glinted in the workhouse master's eyes made Felix move subtly closer to Andrew, who looked down at him. He crouched down, cool gaze studying the boy's features. "I'm sorry it took me so long to get here. Frank's letters stopped and by the time I got back to America and was able to send a telegram, it was already too late. It took me some time to find out where you'd been sent."

Felix didn't think he'd ever been so relieved to see such an unkempt face. "It doesn't matter," he whispered, his eyes shining with his tears.

"Shall we get out of here?" Andrew asked him. Felix nodded with a smile.

"Wait right there, Mr Huxley," Mr Thomas spluttered, "you can't just barge in here and take a child. There are procedures in place. He's been put in my care."

Andrew angled his head. "Care? You call this *care*? Look at his face!"

"He's been a trouble-maker from the beginning,"

Matron said brusquely, "fighting and causing a ruckus in a happy home!"

"Look," Mr Thomas interrupted the tirade that Andrew looked set to release on the woman behind him. "We are happy to reunite families, though we should be compensated for the food and clothing that we have provided for the boy…"

"You want me to buy his release?" Andrew's incredulous voice climbed.

"It's only fair,"

Andrew made a sound of disgust as he scattered a handful of coins across the master's desk and then he scooped Felix up and straight-armed his way through the doors of the workhouse, before setting him into the carriage that was outside the front door.

Andrew caught his chin to study the black eye more closely. "You and me, kid. I don't know how it'll work but I promise you'll not get one of these from me."

Felix sniffed. "They threw my ankh in the fire. They called me a devil worshipper. It's gone, I tried to tell them I'd made a promise to wear it always, Andrew. I'm really sorry."

Andrew's nostrils pinched white as he inhaled sharply. "Wait right here."

The stones crunched under his feet as he stalked back into the workhouse interior. Felix held his breath as he watched the doors close. His eyes skimmed the austere exterior, and he knew that he wouldn't let himself think of his life here. He'd grown to accept that he would never leave and now, Andrew was here to save him. He'd like to believe that Frank had sent him, that he had a guardian angel.

Andrew emerged again, his expression furious as he barked an order to the driver to get them from here and the door of the carriage was slammed behind him. Felix watched this furious man, his eyes fearful as the carriage careened down the drive, away from the workhouse. Andrew took his handkerchief and applied it to his bloody knuckles, breathing heavily. When he saw the boy cowering in the corner away from him, he shook his head.

"I'll get you a new ankh, Felix. You've no reason to fear me. Please, come here, you can tell me what's happened," he gestured him forward and patted the bench next to him. "You can show me where my brother is buried. You'll never be alone again."

CHAPTER 11

*T*rixie

"You shouldn't be smoking in here," Trixie quipped, turning away to set the lamp on the chest of drawers as trepidation hummed along her veins. The lamp clattered against the wooden surface, and she balled her hands into fists and pressed them to her thighs to stem the trembling. She'd often wondered if George would be the one to track her down. Never in her wildest thoughts had she thought Stella would be the one. "You're a long way from London,"

Stella laughed raucously. "Is that all you have to say to me, girl? Not 'Hi, Stella, how's things' or 'how's my sister'? Or even 'sorry, I've been missing for six months, and you've had to drag your sorry backside halfway across the country in a bid to find me'."

Trixie wiped her palms on her skirt and smiled faintly.

"Maybe that should have told you that I didn't want to be found."

Stella's thin brow arched high, and she took a drag from her cigarette, exhaled slowly. "You think I'm going to let my best girl go without saying 'goodbye'?"

"I'm not coming back," Trixie said quickly, darting a glance to the two men who flanked her. Neither she recognised, and she wondered what had happened to George, Billy, John, Maisie…. She wasn't prepared for the onslaught of yearning for the mismatched family that she had known. She had spent the last six months just trying to get by, keeping her head down. "How's Lily?"

"Why did you run?" Stella countered.

Trixie folded her arms and met the stare head on, unflinchingly.

Stella's mouth twisted into a knowing smile. "A little bird tells me that you were in love. What did you do, Trixie? Confess all and he rejected you?"

She couldn't help the flicker of pain that crossed her face and Stella's grin widened.

"You think you're the first of my girls to let some man under their skin?" She shook her head and uncrossed her ankles. "You're not, and you won't be the last. He wasn't worthy of you, Trixie. That much I do know,"

Trixie tucked a strand of hair behind her ears and cleared her throat. "How did you find me?"

Admiration tinged her tone as she shifted in her chair, took another drag on her cigarette. "It was hard, I must admit. What did you do, go legitimate for a while? Get a real job? To prove to yourself that your man had you pegged all wrong?"

Trixie dropped her gaze, wondering how Stella knew all of this. She bobbed her head once, wretchedness pressing down on her. "I really tried. I thought that I was doing it. Got me a job in a factory, without references. Just talked my way into it. Found this place but then the winter came, everyone got laid off. One day, I had spent my last ha'penny and I was starving. I saw a man walking. He was easy picking. The next thing I knew, I was at the pawnshop selling the watch I'd stolen," Trixie noticed how Stella stiffened slightly. "It was that, wasn't it? You had the pawnshops watched? That's how you found me."

She flicked the ash onto the floor. "Yes, Miss Clever Clogs. Actually, I was looking for a young girl selling diamonds, which was what made me send out messages to the shops in the first place. A nice little reward for any information and voila – I found you."

She'd kept the diamonds hidden away. Knew that it would bring unwanted attention to her if she'd tried to sell them. But watches? Rings? They were easy to fence. "I didn't take the diamonds – I told that to Anna until I was blue in the face."

Stella lifted a shoulder. "Well, we searched this room when we found you – they're not anywhere here. After all these years, there is very little in this life that surprises me," She extended a long, elegant finger and her eyes glinted dangerously. "We had an agreement, Trixie. Your sister's safety for your co-operation. You swore to me that you would do whatever it takes. In fact, I think your phrase was "whatever I asked". You were hidden away in that place because it was in the middle of nowhere – in a tiny village, on a genuine job – away from anything to do with Anna and the scrutiny that came after robbing from the duke. I had an inkling that you might enjoy the reprieve a little too much and I thought I'd see what you'd do. Mildred was sent to bring you back after I'd taken steps to make sure you wouldn't get arrested. Mildred told me that you were reluctant to steal from the family, that you'd fallen for a boy, and that you'd gone soft. That cost me money, Beatrix. I thought I was *protecting* you." Her voice climbed higher, and she inhaled sharply, reining in her temper. "I took you both in, I gave your sister a home, all at a great personal cost."

"Is she okay?"

Stella sniffed, handing the expired cigarette to one of the men. "I wanted to punish you by punishing her, but unlike you, she has achieved everything that has been put in front of her. She hasn't let me down. She doesn't deserve to see her sister whom she idolises reduced to this state."

"I'm sorry," Trixie said meekly. "I didn't want to be a thief any longer,"

Stella spread her hands wide in a mocking motion. "And yet, here you are, going back to what you do best. Living in basic accommodation, picking up scraps and living like a pauper,"

"How is this any different to scrubbing floors and getting hit with rolling pins by housekeepers? I was sick of living that way, of living a lie," Trixie exclaimed, exasperated. "At least, this way I'm living on my terms. Making *my* way in the world…"

Stella cast a contemptuous look about the space. "Is this what you want, Trixie? To just get by in life? I can give you so much more. I can make you rich. You've done your time in the small leagues. Look at you! You're growing into a fine-looking woman. You're no longer young enough to pass as a scullery maid, you've done your time in the ranks. I have bigger plans for you." Stella pressed to her feet and crossed to where Trixie was leaning on the drawers. She pulled Trixie upright. "Did he break your heart?" she asked gently, gentle enough to break the barricade around the pain that shrouded Trixie's. A sob escaped her throat, and she covered her face with her hands, nodding. "Good." Stella said gloating.

Trixie's hands dropped away, as she stared at her boss. "'*Good*'? Why is it good to have someone throw you away like you're nothing?"

"I knew that if I left you there long enough, you would fall in love with some helpless languisher. Your sister Angela did it," she shrugged, "stands to reason that you would do the same."

"You knew?"

Stella laughed. "How else was I to teach you to not allow anyone in? You are not to trust anyone, least of all some hapless sap. Men are not worthy of your tears, Trixie. Of course, had I known you'd bolt, I would have sent someone earlier to pull you out. You slipped on by me – that won't happen again. Now, are you ready to come back to work?"

She shook her head in disbelief. "That was a plan, all along? To teach me a lesson?"

Stella dismissed her shrill tone with a wave of her hands. "There's no need to get snippy. Come on, the cab is downstairs waiting. We've got work to do... unless you want to get the diamonds before you leave?"

"And if I say 'no'?"

Stella lowered her head so that their noses were aligned. "Then my bias towards Lily ends. And you know what that means," she ground out through gritted teeth. "Get. Yourself. In. The. Carriage."

Trixie didn't even look back. She had no clothes, no belongings, nothing of significance. She shot down the stairs, past a protesting Agnes, ignoring her worried questions. Instead, Trixie kept her chin high and her shoulders back. Had she really thought that she could make it on her own? Stella owned her, just like she'd owned George for all of these years. Her step faltered as she saw George, lounging against the carriage door. His guarded gaze watched her though he remained mute as he opened the carriage door. With her hand on the edge, Trixie paused with one foot on the lowest rung of the steps. Maisie waited in the corner of the interior, dressed smartly with her hair coiffed neatly.

"In!" Stella pressed a hand to her back and followed her up the steps. Maisie broke the look, turning her head to look out onto the deserted street. The door was closed on the carriage and Trixie accepted the blanket that was handed to her.

"How long will it take to get back to London?"

Stella settled the heavy cover over her knees, smoothing out the material before her eyes swept up, a knowing smile flirting with her lips. "Who said anything about going to London? We're all off on an adventure."

Trixie glanced between them both, though neither woman met her look of incredulity. "You're coming with me?"

"I don't trust you not to run again."

"Where are we going?"

"America," Maisie replied, not looking at her.

"What? Why are we going there? What about Lily?"

Stella sighed, leaned her head back on the plush seat, and closed her eyes. "George is right. You ask too many questions."

$\sim$

FELIX

"WHAT ARE we to do with you, Felix Huxley?"

Felix couldn't help the grin that split his face. Chocolate icing ringed his mouth, the half-eaten sponge cake sitting on the table between the two of them. They were in a hotel, with other guests sat about chatting under the warm glow of the huge chandelier.

"Do you still want to be a doctor?"

Felix shrugged, rubbing an absent hand over his protesting belly and suppressed a gluttonous burp. His mind was a blur of the past few days. He'd told Andrew about Florence and how she'd ransacked Frank's house, burned his books, and pilfered his personal belongings for items to sell before she'd dumped Felix at the workhouse.

They'd visited pompous men in tweed suits to speak about the legalities of what had happened to Frank's belongings before they'd arrived in the noisy, calamitous bedlam of London. He'd been fascinated by the sights of buildings that seemed to lean on each other for support, the smells of roasted meat and dung that melded together into a cacophony that didn't seem to relent, no matter the time of the day. It was a long way from the cruel stillness of the workhouse.

He drained his glass of milk as he contemplated the question. Medicine fascinated him, it was true, but he realised now that he must have tucked away his dreams of a better life. Did he still want to go to school to learn? He loved to learn, that much he knew, but he didn't want to leave the protection of his rescuer. At least, not yet.

Andrew had been succinct in his command of those around him, which hadn't been seen by Felix when they'd last been in London. Andrew had been trimmed, shaved, and spruced up, making him presentable in company once more. The fact that he'd torn up the county looking for Felix would forever be an image that he would hold dear. Felix's eyes dropped to the rock that Andrew was currently rolling back and forth across his knuckles, before it disappeared into his large palm, only to pop out through fingers and begin the path again.

"What's that?"

Andrew gave a start then held the rock out to Felix. "It's a diamond,"

Felix took the rock, grey with black speckles, and flints of red flashing through it. He thought of the clear sparkling stone that he knew to be a diamond. "No, it's not," Felix laughed. "It's a rock."

Andrew's lips curved. "That's how it comes out of the ground – well, I found that one in a river. It's called an alluvial deposit when found like that. You'd called that a diamond in the rough." He scooted closer to the boy. "See those red bits? That's garnet, and quite often they're found together as they're made from similar minerals."

"I thought you collected insects?" Felix puzzled, angling a look towards Andrew.

"I do," Andrew winked. "But I just happen to find the insects near rivers and in caves near where you can find these little rocks, too."

Felix rotated the rock between his fingers, angled it so that the light bounced off it. He couldn't quite envision the precious gem that women wore on their fingers coming from such an ugly-looking thing. "What do you do with it?"

"I'll take it to a lapidary who will cut the stone, then we have a finished product to sell to the highest bidder. Insect collecting is a natural by-product of what I do. Or, at least that's what I tell most people – including my family." Andrew rubbed a hand over his mouth as he contemplated his young ward. Then, he leaned forward, resting the hand on the table. Slowly, he smiled. "Do you want to take a trip, Felix?"

~

FELIX

STOMACH ROLLING, Felix stood on the dockside, though could have sworn that the ground kept swaying in the same motion as the water he'd just spent months on. The air was hot and dusty, and all around him, dark-tanned men and scrawny boys with bare, sandy feet clambered along the quayside. It was pandemonium though he was thankful to be off the boat that had been his home for what felt like a lifetime. Whilst he'd been excited to travel, being cooped up on a small sailboat had soon got tiresome.

Felix stayed close to Andrew as he negotiated his way through the throng of people and stacks of cases and trunks that were littered about where passengers disembarked. Felix liked the fact that Andrew only travelled with his knapsack. It meant that they didn't have to wait around in this heat.

"Are we here now?" Felix asked when Andrew drew up short on the road. Small buildings, squat and beige, lined the streets. Men in long skirts and sandals milled about them and Felix tried not to stare.

"Are you going to keep asking the same question over and over?" Andrew asked without looking at him, though the hand that squeezed his shoulder eased the clipped tone. "I'm looking for my contact. I told him we'd be here, though he'll probably be in a watering hole here some-where. Are you hungry?"

Felix shook his head, blowing out his breath to try and lift his fringe that clung to his damp forehead. "I'm hot," he tugged on his collar.

Andrew took in the woollen trousers that were now almost short length on Felix and the heavy tunic shirt. "I bet you are. Let's get you kitted out with some suitable attire. You're dressed for London, not south-east Asia."

"We don't have any money," Felix said, having to trot to keep up with Andrew's long strides.

Andrew looked up and down the road before they ducked into a narrow doorway. Felix was puzzled as Andrew turned his back to the road and then he realised that Andrew was shielding what he was doing from prying eyes. He took out a pouch, like the one that the ankh had been in when he'd been given it.

"You don't always need money in life, Felix." Andrew took the boy's hand and opened his palm before he upended the pouch. Tiny stones of blood red, royal blue, deep green, and sparkling white plopped into the centre of his hand. Felix peered at them, touched them gently with his fingertip, admiring the way the light refracted as they rotated their sharp edges across his skin.

"What is it you do again?" he frowned.

Andrew lowered his voice as he opened the pouch wider and indicated that Felix should put the gemstones back in. "I facilitate deals."

"What does that mean?"

Andrew ruffled his hair. "You're about to get a whole different education, Felix."

PART II

Five Years Later

CHAPTER 12

⁂

*T*rixie

FOG CLUNG TO THE DOCKS, the ship's masts looming like spectres in the morning mists, giving an ethereal feel to the day. Gull's cries filled the salty air. Trixie emerged onto the gangway and took a moment to inhale.

"Smell that, Maisie? God, I've missed it,"

Maisie nudged her in the back, urging her down the walkway. "It stinks. It's cold and it's damp. How can you miss something so ugly and smelly?"

Trixie laughed, turning once she reached the quay. "What can I say? I'm a Londoner. I can't wait to hear a bit of the mother tongue!"

"At least one of us is glad to be back!" Maisie squinted along each way, then lifted her hand when she saw a porter. She directed him to the luggage and handed him a coin then she turned back towards Trixie, her eyes searching the crowds milling about them. "Someone is meant to be meeting us outside here. God, it's freezing! I miss the New York sunshine already."

Trixie snorted. "It was raining when we left America. And you should have fetched a coat from your luggage."

Maisie planted her hands on her hips, not caring that she was blocking the path of the other passengers as they scrambled for their belongings. "You're awfully chipper for someone who's been trapped in that tin can boat for weeks."

Trixie slung her arm around Maisie's shoulders and laughed gaily. The porter loaded their trunks onto a trolley and they followed him as he dragged it along the quay towards the exit. "It's a luxury liner, and did we not have the best suite on there?"

"Thanks to you and that card game – that you nearly lost, by the way!"

"The keyword there is 'nearly'. And I didn't. I had that gorgeous Lord whatever-his-name-was right where I wanted him,"

Maisie wriggled out from her friend's grip. "Well, there was no mistaking where he wanted *you* to be. I don't know how you managed to keep him panting after you for so long. There was absolutely nothing wrong with the room that we had been assigned. We were told to keep our heads down and come back into the country quietly, and ready to work,"

Trixie shrugged. "Stella left over a year ago – and travelling bores me," she bumped her shoulder into her friend. "Besides, I have to hone my skills, you know – stay sharp."

Maisie pinned her with a look. "You have an answer for everything, Trixie White."

Trixie schooled her face into one of contrition but couldn't maintain it for longer than a second before she collapsed into a fit of giggles. Maisie stomped off, annoyance coming off her in waves, ignoring Trixie's shouts to wait for her.

When Trixie spotted the familiar face amongst the carriages that blocked the road at the gates of the docks, she stopped and waited for him to meet her gaze. He still wore the same cap and looked smartly dressed in his black woollen coat and trousers, a cigarette dangling from his mouth. She knew the moment he'd spotted them as he straightened, his surprise sliding to a slow grin that moved across his face. He removed his cap, yanked the cigarette down, his eyes sparkling as he watched her approach. His companion jumped down from the cab and dismissed the youngster away from the cases, began loading them up.

"Aren't you a sight for sore eyes? Look at you!"

Trixie dipped a mocking curtsy for him. Her hair was twisted up into an elegant curl, some of which artfully tumbled out to frame her face. "Hello, George,"

"You've grown up,"

She patted his cheek, ignoring the deep, angry-looking scar that marred his left eye and cheek. "It's been a while. How have you been?"

"You know me, kid. American looks like it suited you," He opened his arms and she stepped into his embrace.

"Hard work and time to come home," She squeezed him and then stepped back. "How have things been?"

He winked. "You need to ask the boss, not me."

"And Lily?"

He set the box down and opened the door for them both, handing first Maisie and then Trixie into the carriage. He shut the door, fingers curving over the edge as he peered through the open window. "Looking forward to seeing you again."

He vanished from the doorway, thumping could be heard as he stowed the box and climbed up next to the driver.

"Did you see that scar?" Maisie whispered. "Is that what he got from the Bazey boys' trouble?"

Trixie tugged on the fingertips of her gloves. "Probably," she said in a tight voice so as not to be heard. "I know it was a scrap and a half. We lost a few good men that night. He could have lost an eye," She folded the gloves, laid her hands in her lap, and tried not to dwell on what she was coming back to. The last time she was here, she was only a tiny cog in a very big wheel, so she hadn't been as involved in the darker side of the belly of this vibrant city.

"I suppose it beats shimmying down a drainpipe and having to lie flat on the shingles until the shift change at the local bobby shop, though," Maisie smirked. "You were so mad that night."

"It was freezing and bloody raining cats and dogs,"

Trixie tried to sound annoyed, but her lips twitched. "Got the job done though, didn't I?"

"You always do."

"I half-expected Stella to meet us," Trixie said quietly, her attention drawn outside as the London scene raced past in a blur.

"She's probably busy. You've seen the telegrams – business is brisk. She's fighting for territory and supremacy. It's not like you're going to run again,"

Trixie smiled because she knew that was what was expected of her. Those few stolen months in Manchester seemed like they had happened to a different person now, as did the vague images of the man who'd asked her to marry him. Now, she had business figures and dates rolling around her mind. She'd embraced her new life in the new world. She'd worked to be the best. And just as Stella had foretold, she had been rewarded in riches. Sometimes, she missed the innocence of the time when she had thought that she could survive in this world without doing what she did best. Other times, her naivety amused her endlessly. "No, I won't run again. Also, that joke is beyond old, now."

"About as old as George is looking," Maisie sniggered, and Trixie shook her head ruefully. London, with its sights and smells, drifted through the windows, and she was hit with a sense of homesickness that had been missing from her life for so long.

"It's good to be back," she remarked, and she hoped that she was right.

～

"You promise that you'll still be here tomorrow?" Lily asked, a tinge of apprehension in her voice.

Trixie returned the hug of her little sister, her eyes twinkling warmly. "I will be here, I promise."

"Then, I shall bid you goodnight," Lily dipped her head, the skirts of her dress whispering as she left the room.

"I shall send Ethel up to aid Miss Lily and ready her for bed," the butler murmured and exited the room.

Trixie's brows climbed her forehead and she turned to face Stella who was lounging in a highbacked chair similar to the one she'd been in the first time Trixie had negotiated with her. "She has a maid?"

"Of course," Stella scoffed, "I have big plans for my girl. She'll go far in life. She needs to get used to certain advantages of living with servants, especially after she has her 'coming out to the society' party. Oh, what a picture she'll look."

Trixie rose to disguise her churning jealousy and crossed to the drink's cabinet that was rosewood, in keeping with the ostentatious furniture that Stella had selected to fill her extravagant home with. She'd thought that George had brought her straight to the first job when the carriage had rolled up outside the grand entrance of the townhouse, with its ornate wrought iron fence and pristinely swept steps rising to a glossy front door and brass knocker. Her shock had quickly turned to joy when she'd caught a glimpse of a vibrant, healthy-looking girl who held vague likeness to her mother waiting for her in the doorway. Lily had certainly grown into a pretty young lady, with deportment and impeccable manners, the likes of which she may never have had if they'd done as Angela had instructed all those years ago, and ran from the hovel that they'd lived in.

She'd listened to Lily's stories during dinner of school and her friends with a peculiar mix of pride and envy. Her sister hadn't ever scrubbed a floor, or emptied a chamber pot, but nor had she had to fend off unwanted attentions of a drunk and amorous man. Trixie knew how to inflict pain if she had to; she also knew men who, for a coin and a pint, would dispatch that man into a hole in the ground.

She took a crystal glass and sloshed a hefty dose of brandy into it – uncaring that it was the expensive type, for when Stella entertained. Trixie turned back to the room and glanced about. Damask-patterned material covered the walls in rich burgundy, the soft light from the wall sconces making the gilt-framed oil paintings gently gleam. Fresh cut flowers bloomed from elegant vases on tables and sideboards as the fire crackled merrily in the huge, black fireplace that dominated the far wall.

"Your home is fancy," Trixie commented, lifting the glass to her lips. "A far cry from the warehouse."

Stella's smile didn't quite reach her eyes. "Would you rather stay there tonight? It can be arranged, though my girls are in better accommodation across town now. The warehouse has gone back to storage use."

"And what are we storing there these days?"

"You ran the New York side of things – you leave the London one up to me."

Trixie sipped her drink, enjoying the heat that blazed down her gullet and bloomed in her belly. "I did run it – successfully, I might add. Set it up and put the best people in the right places. Pulled off jobs that men wouldn't even dream of," Trixie's eyes gleamed in the light, her voice tinged with gratification. "I did everything that was asked of me, and more. I didn't think that I would ever come back here. When you left, you'd put me in charge and I figured that that was my lot – and I was happy having some independence, with growing a good team of my own. I had a life there; I made the both of us money." She took another drink before she aimed the glass at Stella, who nodded. Trixie refilled her glass, poured Stella a drink, and carried it across the plush gold and red carpet. She held the glass just out of reach and asked, "so why the hell am I back here?"

Stella merely held her hand out and waited for Trixie to set the glass into her grasp. Stella swirled the amber liquid in the glass, watching the light playing through it. Trixie held back the sigh and moved towards the fire. She rested an elbow on the mantle as she watched the flames dance and lick their way across the coal.

"In the four years that we worked New York, I had to play both sides of the water. You know what it's like – those sharks out there sense a chink in the armoury and they're on the hunt for blood," Stella's voice was calmly detached. Trixie didn't move, even though she knew that tone to be her deadly one, and her skin puckered with goosebumps. "Growing the business there meant I was able to teach you the ropes. How to hire the best tricksters, putters-up, cracksman…"

"It's why they call you the queen of thieves," Trixie replied.

Stella husked a laugh and Trixie heard the click of her swallow, then the glass being set into the small table next to her chair. "I won't be the queen for always, my dearest Beatrix,"

Trixie did look up then, a frown wrinkling her forehead. Sharp eyes took in the elegant woman. Finest cloth covered her, diamonds sparkled on her fingers and a fat emerald was nestled at the V of her throat. "Where are you going?"

Stella rested her chin on her curved fingers, her index finger extended up her cheek. "I can escape most things, except death, Beatrix. I want a finer life. I have this house; I have powerful friends high up…"

"You want more." Trixie's mind began to spin, wondering what her angle was this time. Because there was always an angle with this woman.

Stella pulled a face as her shoulder lifted. "Naturally,"

"And what else is there? You have this house, staff, money, power."

"I don't have status. I will always be that scrubber from Spitalfields who grew up poor and chasing rats. Lily may have had a start just around the corner from mine, but I have made sure that she won't remember that life. Only the best for my girl."

Trixie straightened, and awareness trickled down her

spine as she saw an emotion cross the face of the illustrious Stella. *Pride.* She was proud of her young ward, Lily. She wanted her to fit into society. She had educated her, kept her away from the business, coddled and preened. *Her coming-out party.* Where, at the height of the season, Lily would have a party just in her name. She could imagine that Lily would slot right into the upper class of the society, looking perfect on the arm of a prince or a duke…

"How long have you had this place?" Trixie asked, kept her face impassive.

"Five years,"

The duke. The blackmail. *Was that how she'd paid for this place?*

"Why do you ask?"

"You've come a long way in the past five years, Stella. I think there are a few more years in you just yet," Trixie saluted her with her glass, drained the contents, as she pushed through her tumultuous thoughts. She didn't want to think of her innocent sister as a pawn in one of Stella's cons. Perhaps her greatest con. "But you haven't answered my question. Why am I here?"

Stella straightened, folded her hands in her lap, and her mouth curved up in a crocodilian smile. "Because I need a safe breaking – and you are the best one that I know."

CHAPTER 13

*T*rixie

"CAN you believe that they have a *maid* serving food?" the old man to Trixie's right grumbled to his companion, "Whatever next!"

"It's shameful," the woman agreed, "the whole world is going quite mad. I never would have had our host pegged as one of those dreadful people in favour of the vote."

Trixie sipped at her wine and tried to ignore the conversation that he'd spent more than half of the evening trying to draw her into. They were seated at a huge oval table, and the chatter of a social evening flowed, interspersed with the clink of glass and tinkle of haughty laughter. Trixie had gone through the motion of the evening, her mind on the job at hand. Not for the first time tonight, she'd had an itch between her shoulder blades as if she was being watched. She trusted her gut and had tried to locate the source of what was making her feel uncomfortable without making it obvious.

Maisie was fully engaged on the other side of the table, playing the role of a dutiful addition on the arm of one of the guests, and avoiding looking at Trixie just like she was meant to. Surreptitiously, Trixie scanned the table again. This time, she was met with the cool grey gaze of the handsome stranger. She'd not noticed him before but instinctively she knew that he was the source of this unsettled feeling. Even from this distance, she felt the jolt of being the centre of his attention deep in her belly as something visceral unfurled within her. He lifted his glass in a small toast. It took everything in her not to react – to do something over how he'd affected her.

"What say you, my dear?" the old man leaned in and murmured in her ear.

Trixie, annoyed by both her reaction and offended by the man's odious-smelling breath, turned on him, smiling sweetly. "Don't you think that women are capable of more than just filling your bed, sir?"

Trixie heard the audible gasp of the pious woman who'd been in agreement with him and immediately wanted to bite back her words. She always tried not to be memorable at these types of events – in her line of work, it didn't pay to be noticed. Now, she'd caused outrage, and would no doubt be the subject of many a conversation, even if they only knew her by the alias she'd given when she'd arrived.

"You're one of *those*, are you?" the old man sneered,

rearing back as if she'd bitten him. "Your type get every-where and will be the downfall of our grand nation, mark my words,"

Time to go, Trixie thought and turned her attention to forcing Maisie to make her move.

~

FELIX

RIGHT UP UNTIL the moment that he saw her, Felix had decided to cut the evening short. He detested events like this, where the banal chatter and the social small talk bored him to tears, but it was a necessary evil for being successful in his line of business. He'd mentally berated Andrew for ducking out on what was his turn to strike the deal and sending him in his place, until the woman had walked in the room, dressed in a deep purple gown that made the sapphire of her eyes more vivid and with her lustrous brown hair twisted up off the nape of her long neck.

She was the most attractive woman in the room. Certainly, perhaps, the most attractive woman he'd ever seen. He'd watched her from across the room, as she moved around, and was curious to see that while she answered everybody who spoke with her, she was ever watchful of the space that she was in and didn't really seem present. Indeed, during his covert observations, he noticed that whilst she appeared to eat and drink, the level of food and drink that she consumed didn't go down.

And then when he'd finally caught her eye, she'd been almost dismissive of him. She'd almost looked through him. The dismissal was an unfamiliar feeling. Whilst he wasn't an arrogant man, he knew from experience that women liked how he looked, and he never failed to secure a female companion for a social event, though considering how much he'd travelled, it was never conducive to settling down or getting married. He could see the flash of annoyance that crossed her expression as the old man murmured something in her ear. Judging by the gentleman's response, he could see that her reply had been as taut as her expression. He wondered what her response had been to cause such offence.

"Excuse me," Felix murmured to the young lady on his left. The woman preened under his look, though her sultry expression was short-lived when Felix asked, "Do you happen to know the name of the woman sat over there? The one in the purple dress,"

"Mary? Margaret – something like that. She is new in town, from America. She's an associate of one

of the partners in the company, I believe." The woman replied, coolly.

Felix gave her a warm smile and watched as she seemed to come back to life under it. He stifled a sigh. No wonder the other beauty had piqued his interest when she'd not even reacted to him. He made a vow to seek her out before the end of the night before the men and women divided for cigars and gossip.

"America? Have you ever been?"

When she replied, his mind wandered. If she was an American, she might be bored and happy to speak to someone who'd travelled America extensively. He'd been back in London for almost a week here to do business. Andrew had promised that their stopover in the city would only be a brief sojourn before they went travelling again. Striking the type of deal like he had done tonight was the necessary evil of what they did for a living. He didn't enjoy it. However, it meant that he could live a comfortable lifestyle whilst seeing some of the world that had fascinated him since he was a small boy.

It was then that the shrill scream pierced the air. Felix's eyes were drawn, along with every other occupant in the room as one of the guests crumpled to the floor, dragging the plate and cutlery off the table in a dead faint. The accompanying gasps and cries to such an event as people rushed to the aid of the woman who'd fainted drew his attention momentarily.

"Make room! Give her some air!" One of the more esteemed men cried, who Felix assumed to be a doctor as he edged the crowd back that had circled the girl on the floor.

Felix heard the soft moan as she started to come to, and he lifted his lips in a rueful smile as he heard her claim that she'd seen a mouse, followed by her profuse apologies for having caused a scene. He thought about the critters and rodents that he'd found clambering over him over the years. He knew that the type of people he shared the table with tonight wouldn't have the stomach for such things. Unlike most guests, Felix hadn't moved from his seat. However, when he looked again down the table, his object of attention had gone.

$$\backsim$$

TRIXIE

TRIXIE HURRIED ALONG THE LANDING, keeping back in the shadows whilst keeping a half-ear open as she listened for the distraction that Maisie was meant to cause downstairs. She'd committed the map of the house to memory, the information having been supplied by the young maid serving food tonight that Stella had planted to get the layout of the house and the location of the safe.

Normally, she didn't gain access to a job through the front door, though she wasn't sure that clambering over rooftops and shimmying down drainpipes was preferable to being caught red-handed in all her finery as a dinner guest. She counted down the doors and let a whispered curse when the door was locked.

The maid had assured her that the door was always left open. *This is going to lose precious minutes,* she thought crossly as she slipped a hand inside her bodice and pulled out her lockpicking set. Within moments, the lock gave a satisfying click as it slid back. Allowing herself a satisfied smile, she glanced down the empty hallway and slipped inside the room. She waited for her eyes to adjust in the darkness, her heart in her throat. She crossed the room on her tiptoes and pulled the small picture frame off the wall, giving a shake of her head as the safe came into view.

"You make this too easy," she whispered and checked the lock of the safe. That part at least was correct, though it was the more difficult type to crack. She went to work, her nimble fingers using the tools that she'd hidden in the skirts of her grand dress. Just when she wondered if she was going to run out of time, Trixie heard the resounding crash of a tray hitting the floor downstairs. The maid that they'd planted would have dropped it in the middle of the dining room if she wasn't back in the room by the time Maisie was on her feet. Trixie gave a grin as the safe door popped open.

It always paid to have a back-up plan.

∼

FELIX

"LEAVING SO SOON?"

Up close, she was even more beautiful, and Felix felt the effect of her bemused look as she turned back to him deep in his gut. He'd been looking for her since the fiasco at dinner and had caught a brief glimpse of her heading out of the room as she requested her coat from one of the footmen. When he found himself gawping, her expression cooled, and she dismissed him as she tried to step around him. Undeterred, he countered by matching her move and couldn't stop from drinking in his fill of her; she had a light dusting of freckles over her upturned nose, full lips and he could see her pulse pounding above a particularly beautiful Tanzanite stone. *Now, just where did an American socialite source such a rare gemstone?*

"I'm afraid that I'm rarely in the mood for frivolity, as one finds with these after-dinner events when women occupy their time discussing who is stepping out with whom," she replied in a briskly tart tone.

Not an American, he thought and gave her his most winning smile. "A girl after my own heart. I don't believe we've met. Felix Huxley," he stuck his hand out. She merely stared at his hand, and he laughed, leaning forward to whisper, "This is usually the part where you tell me your name, Miss...?"

The chatter behind them drew her attention. The young girl, who'd made a spectacle of herself when she'd fainted was still apologising to their hosts, whilst being assisted to the front door by her amorous suitor. If he wasn't quite so aware of the mysterious woman, he might have missed the flicker of relief that rippled over her face before the distant mask was back in place.

"Goodnight, sir," she said quickly and shot through the door as it was opened to let the other woman out. Felix wanted to follow her out, though his manners dictated that he stand back to allow the chattering girl through. As he did, he saw the object of his attention being handed into a waiting carriage by a dangerous-looking man with a deep scar on his face. Now, what kind of a woman would hire a deeply disfigured man, especially one who emanated danger as if it pumped in his veins. Instead of giving up, Felix was now more interested in her than ever.

~

TRIXIE

"FELIX HUXLEY IS BACK IN TOWN," Maisie informed the room casually the following morning.

"Is he as handsome as I remember?" Stella's eyes gleamed.

Maisie's brows danced. "Better, though you might want to ask Trixie, as they seemed very cosy in the doorway together last night."

Trixie eye rolled when both women looked at her. "His attention was on you and your ridiculously dramatic performance, as was the plan."

Maisie's eyes sparkled with mischief. "They spoke," she informed Stella pointedly.

"What did he say to you?"

Trixie had spent the night tossing and turning, disturbed by dreams of grey eyes chasing her through endless hallways. She'd left her hotel room that morning intending to take a stroll along the streets, but her plans had been curtailed when one of Stella's men had been waiting for her at the street, having been sent to collect her.

Trixie made a non-committal face, ever aware of the speculation as Stella looked at her. "He merely introduced himself, no time for anything more before Maisie was leaving. I was trying to extricate myself with the loot so was keen to escape in case the staff raised the alarm."

"Was Andrew Huxley with him?"

"No, he was alone."

Trixie had heard of the two Huxley's, their notoriety of buying and selling the higher quality end of gemstones had reached both shores of the Atlantic. Though, until last night, she'd not given either of them a second thought. Until last night, no man had ever looked at her in such a manner, as if she was the last morsel of food on a plate and he was a starving man.

"I must find out what they're in town for," Stella murmured, straightening in her chair, seemingly satisfied with Trixie's answers. "I'm sure you'd have the cream of the crop if you were to burgle their hotel suite."

"That's true – the quality of the stones that they deal with is legendary, though they're never in town for long." Maisie supplied.

Stella tapped a fingertip to her lips, and Trixie could almost hear the cogs of her business mind turning. "I've tried to get close to Andrew over the years but he's much too canny for me. They rarely deal with the same jeweller, nor do they ever reside at the same hotels. That's what makes them harder to track."

"I've never heard of either of them being the victim of a theft," said Maisie, lips twitching.

Trixie lowered her cup, dividing a look between them. "Don't even think about it. I'm not doing it."

Stella grinned. "I don't believe that those words are in my vocabulary. Besides... if anyone can do it, you can."

Trixie opened her mouth to argue but knew from the look of Stella that any debating would be futile. She drained her cup to keep her expression neutral, dismay making her coffee swirl nauseously at the thought of seeing Felix Huxley again.

CHAPTER 14

Felix

"I MET A GIRL LAST NIGHT."

For the first time since joining Andrew at breakfast, the older man lowered the corner of his newspaper to spear Felix with a look. "You never say that. Anyone I know?"

Felix easily conjured up her face in his mind. "She didn't tell me her name."

Andrew's eyes narrowed. Whilst his face had aged from all the years of squinting against the blazing sunlight and was the colour of a ripe conker, his brown gaze was still as sharp. "Then you haven't "met" anyone." He flicked the corner of the paper back into place. Felix waited for a beat before Andrew lowered the paper again. "More beautiful than the Maharaja's daughter?"

Felix grinned unrepentantly as he slathered a pan of butter onto his toast. "She made the Maharaja's daughter pale by comparison."

"And you didn't discover her name? You must be losing your touch, old boy."

Felix chuckled. "I think I must be, Uncle. She looked at me like I was nothing... and I still can't get her out of my mind."

Andrew folded the newspaper, set it alongside his breakfast. Felix had always joined his uncle for breakfast for as long as he could remember. The older man poured himself a coffee, added several sugar cubes. "You did well with the deal last night."

Felix acknowledged the compliment with his slice of bread. "Makes it easier when the buyer has the capital to spend, though I'm not sure I liked talking business before a big meal."

"Maybe the alcohol consumed greased the wheels of finance," Andrew shrugged.

"It was like getting in the bath with my socks on," Felix replied around his food, "I don't care to repeat it."

Andrew chortled. "My dear boy, you are an endless supply of funny anecdotes. You'll be pleased to know that I have booked our tickets to return to Asia. We'll go via America this time. I have business in New York to attend to."

"When do we leave?"

"Tomorrow, so you don't have long to discover the name of your crush. And don't deny it, I can see the excitement in your face like a man who's discovered a

Burmese Ruby as big as a man's fist. Get her out of your system and let's make tracks."

Felix longed to spend his day tracking her down, but the endless tasks of business yawned before him. Andrew loved the exploration and acquisition of their stocks – it was Felix's job to invest the money they made and keep them semi-legal to be classed as legitimate businessmen. "Alas, Uncle, the bank manager calls. Shall I join you for supper?"

Andrew picked up his paper again, his attention distracted by the tedium of business chat. "Certainly, dear boy."

$$\sim$$

TRIXIE

TRIXIE WASN'T sure how Stella had found the information out so fast, though people would generally give up information for a few coins and to gain favour with the gang leader.

In less than a few hours since she'd been having her coffee with her mistress, the job had been set and all the information had come through from one of the staff members at the hotel. Trixie had been tasked with relieving the Huxley's of their jewels, and she tried not to think about how she'd feel about being within the inner sanctum of the Huxley's hotel room.

She emerged from the bowels of the building, dressed in a maid's uniform, with her dark hair tucked up under her bonnet. She hugged the sheets to her chest and made her way towards the service stairs, trotting up them. Whilst a large hotel afforded her some anonymity, robbing a man who haunted every living minute wore her patience thin and she just wanted to get the business over and done with.

The commotion in the lobby as she rounded the corner for the main stairs snared her attention. She nearly hurried on in case she was spotted by the hotel manager when the man who'd been haunting the periphery of her awareness for the past day materialised out of the lift. Though, instead of his impertinent smile, his expression was one of unbridled grief. He sombrely trailed behind a stretcher carrying a body draped in a sheet from the building. Trixie was aware of gasps of shock and dismay that buzzed through the crowd, the cries of horrified women who turned their faces into the shoulders of their husbands to avert the sorrowful scene.

Trixie only had eyes for him. Wordlessly, she turned and made her way back down the stairs, shucking off the maid's uniform so that when she erupted through a side door into the alleyway, she was back in her street clothes and fleeing the scene.

∽

"YOU SURE IT WAS EMPTY? You checked the whole room?"

Trixie made herself sound as affronted as she could. "Either they'd traded everything, or Huxley took everything with him when he followed his uncle out of the hotel. I'm telling you the safe was empty, and he'd not stashed anything in the usual places, though it was hard to check as I didn't have long. How was I to know that the old man would up and croak?"

"You're right," Stella sighed disgruntledly. "The timing couldn't be worse – I was certain we had them this time. Never mind, I have another job for you. I need you to pack. You'll have to take Maisie. She'll be your lady's maid. You're going to the Scottish Highlands."

Trixie acted as if she was paying attention to the instructions whilst she tried to assess if Stella had known that she was lying. She'd ran. She hadn't wanted to do the job and, for the first time in her career, she'd deliberately abandoned a job. There was no doubt that her timing of seeing Felix Huxley following his uncle's body out of the hotel would have been perfect for her to break into his room. But there was something about him that disturbed her, that seeing him in his grief had softened the cage she'd erected around her heart after Morgan. She was glad that Felix had left town. Stella was right. There were always more safes for her to crack. The biggest one of all was the one around her heart.

∽

"Do you ever think about Angela?"

The question startled Trixie and she looked at Lily,

unable to disguise the surprise on her face. Trixie looked behind them, pleased to see that George had done as she'd asked, and allowed them to walk around the park alone. Trixie had been delighted when Lily had begun making attempts to reconnect with her and, since then, they took a walk every Sunday. Occasionally, if Trixie wasn't working, she would take Lily out to tea in one of the city's ever-growing hotel restaurants, like two ladies about town.

"Sometimes," she admitted. "Not so much now I'm older. Why do you ask?"

Lily looked behind her and Trixie frowned. Her sister, usually so vibrant and silly with frivolity, was suddenly serious and appeared so much older. "I'm glad that she got away."

"Is everything okay?"

Lily slipped her hand through her arm, her voice tinged with regret. "When you came home, I was so excited but also scared. I wondered if you were the same sister who'd stepped up to protect me."

Trixie stared at her dumbfounded.

Lily pressed on; her voice low but earnest. "I know what Stella does. I know what you do for her. I don't mind," she added quickly as tears filled Trixie's eyes. "I know that you had no choice as a child. I know that Stella was making herself demented trying to find you that time you tried to run away. I tried to tell myself that you had no choice to go – and now I know that you had no choice but to come back. For me."

"How did you...?"

"People talk, Trixie. And, whilst I might come across as this dotty, polite, society girl..."

"You're still a White, deep down." Trixie finished as Lily's voice tailed off.

Lily laughed and patted her sister's hand. "Exactly."

"So, you've pretended, this whole time?"

"What else was I to do? Stella wanted a daughter – it was apparent to me that I needed to conform to survive."

"Well, Lily White, you certainly had me fooled," Trixie replied admiringly.

"I had to try and get to know you, see what side of the equation you sat on before I showed the real me."

"So, why now?"

"Stella..." Lily hesitated, checked behind her again.

"Stop looking," Trixie reminded her, a fake smile on her face as she curved an arm around her sister's shoulder. "They can't hear us from there and your actions will look suspicious. We're two young women discussing Parisian fashion. That's all,"

"I think that Stella wants to match me to someone. I... I *know* she does," Lily amended.

Trixie lifted a brow in question.

"I picked the lock on her bedroom door," Lily said in a rush.

Trixie didn't think she could be prouder unless she'd taught her sister to pick the lock herself. No doubt her little sister was blessed with the same survival gene that Angela and she had, too.

"I thought I had more time to plan an escape but..." Lily sighed, her voice growing thick with emotion. "She is in correspondence with a Russian who has royal blood. He has proposed marriage and wants to become my husband on my 16th birthday."

"Lily, that's eight months away."

Lily nodded. "I know. I don't want this. I never wanted any of this. I certainly don't want to be shipped off to some foreign land where no one speaks English, or where Stella can tag along as the mother of a Russian princess or whatever I will be. So, Trixie, how did Angela get away? And more to the point, how can we?"

～

THE NEWSPAPER WAS SLAPPED onto the table as Stella swanned past her, leaving a scent of roses and smoke in her wake. Trixie sent the printed page a glance though kept her expression neutral.

"Seen that?"

Trixie crossed her legs and leaned an elbow on the arm of the chair that she was sat in to cup her chin in her hand. Stella took the taller chair on the other side of her mahogany desk. "What of it?"

Stella made a show of lighting her cigarette, extinguished her match, and drew a lungful of smoke before she sent in it a long stream towards the ceiling. "You're getting a name for yourself," She waved a bejewelled finger at the print. "It has a description of you – all that is missing is a photo of you, and it won't be long before someone gives them a detailed enough description, or a photograph of you."

The article detailed many – not all – of the burglaries that Trixie had perpetrated in the last five months and speculated on her identity. She'd read it that morning and had known that this was the reason that Stella had summoned her to the town house before she'd arrived. "This is lazy journalism with complete conjecture. It's nothing that hasn't been printed in the past – the description could be any smartly dressed woman with brown hair in their twenties. It's made the paper because I'm a woman, that's all. Weren't you the one who's always said not to worry until I'm stood in front of a magistrate?"

"Well, I don't care for it. These peelers are getting better at catching criminals – and the people that we're targeting can afford to pay a decent amount for the right information. One of the blighters has even offered a reward,"

"How much am I worth?" Trixie's voice was laced with amused intrigue.

"This isn't a laughing matter. I've managed to keep my neck out of the noose for all these years by staying one step ahead of the police. I told you, I have big plans and I won't have some slum rat on a power trip take me down with her,"

Trixie rolled her eyes even as unease trickled along her spine. "I'll just work outside of London for a while. Maybe not crack any safes – change my method."

"If this carries on, I might have to rethink you going back to America,"

I'm not leaving my sister to your dastardly plans. I need more time for the right job to pay for our travel and a fresh start somewhere else. Trixie gave a slow blink of boredom as Stella smoked a bit more and considered her, eyes squinting against the smoke.

"We should just find someone who looks like you to take the fall. They wouldn't hang a first offender,"

Trixie shook her head, trying to keep her voice level at the horror of the suggestion. *It would be like sending a lamb to slaughter.* "Two months ago, I took money and papers from a magistrate up in Birmingham. Plus, how many members of the peerage have I robbed in the last five months? That's a dreadful idea, Stella – whoever went in the dock in my place would be under the gallows before the judge could shout 'guilty'. I'll be more careful – maybe wait until things die down before my next job."

Stella's face remained motionless except for the slight curving of a brow. "You want to take a holiday?"

"Why not? I've done it before."

"Because you're a thief, Trixie, and this isn't the bloody Brown's hotel." She tapped off her ash, took another drag as she lounged against the high-backed chair, then nodded, her mind made up. "No, you'll return to New York. It's about time someone went back there to check on things as it is. I shall make the arrangements as soon as possible."

Trixie had to bite back the futile rage that filled her. If she left, it would mean that Lily was vulnerable to being sent to meet with her Russian royalty sooner rather than later. Was that Stella's motivation? Had she heard that they'd been meeting up more regularly since Lily had admitted that she too had been keeping up appearances to survive in this criminal life? There was no point in trying to work it out – they were playing a delicate, dangerous game. She had some money saved, but nowhere near enough for two people to relocate. She needed just one big cash job – something that she could liquidate quickly. She would reach out tonight to some of her underground contacts, see what she could shake loose.

"Fine," Trixie replied as she pressed to her feet and buttoned up her coat. "I'd best go and make preparations to pack up my rooms then."

"Trixie?" Stella's voice stopped her before she'd closed the door. Trixie looked back and lifted her chin in response. "This is for the best. I know that Lily will be disappointed, but this won't be forever. I can't afford to lose my best thief, okay?"

Trixie closed the door on Stella's paltry placations, her heels clicking across the parquet flooring. She jogged down the steps and reluctantly climbed into the waiting carriage. What she wanted to do was get on with the task of finding the delinquents of the underworld who would know the best houses to target but walking back to her place now would draw unwanted attention from the driver, especially when she rarely walked anywhere. She needed to tread carefully, now more than ever. Stella never made a rash decision. Something had tipped her hand and Trixie had a feeling it had something to do with the Russian Prince. Her mind raced ahead with ways to get them both out of London before the boat tickets were bought. She always knew that she couldn't do this forever. Until a few months ago, before Lily had trusted her enough to divulge what she'd been through, Trixie had always assumed that she'd either spend her life on the run or finish at the end of the hangman's rope, and that had been okay with her. Now, though, with Lily by her side, she had something left to fight for once more.

CHAPTER 15

Felix

"FANCY SOME COMPANY TONIGHT, DARLIN'? I'll show you how a real woman does it," the prostitute added an exaggerated wink with the suggestion, leaning forward to press her chest at Felix.

"Not tonight, sweetheart," he gave her a wink back before stepping around her. He could hear the rowdy crowds that populated the cellar bar from up on the street level before he'd even taken his first step, but he felt more at home here with the prostitutes and the sailors than he ever did with the politicians and the dukes that frequented the more popular theatres.

He'd been back in London for less than a day and already he could feel his grief pressing in on him once more. Everywhere he looked, there were reminders of the adventures he'd had with Andrew, with Frank. And everywhere he looked, he was reminded of how he'd found them both, their faces slack and grey with death. He'd been reluctant to return but eventually, the insistence of the legal letters from Andrew's solicitor had been too much and Felix had caught a boat back. He'd finalise Andrew's estate, settle their financial affairs before he was able to disappear into the anonymity of the wider world once more.

He gave a nod at the huge man who stood as a sentinel on the door and stepped into the chaos that was a docklands pub. The sounds, the smells, the catcalls, and the bellowing of the punters melded together into a discord that instantly calmed him. He edged his way to the bar, having to push and use his elbows to wedge himself between two huge dockers who reeked of fish, their smocks still stained with whatever they'd unloaded that day. The barman lifted his chin for his order and Felix indicated whisky – bottle – and slid a note across the bar. He nonchalantly met the speculative looks of the dockers, who edged away from him. With his full beard and billy cap pulled low, he snatched the glass and pulled away from the bar, only to stop. Slowly, he pivoted back, trying to see what had snagged his attention within the cesspit of humanity. The crowd waved, shimmied, like the eddying waters of the sea and he saw him, the man with the deeply scarred face that had driven the beauty...

There, as if his mind had finally managed to invoke

her memory into his reality, he saw her. Her hair was simpler than when he'd first seen her, and her eyes looked black in the low light. The group pitched, moved, and Felix had to spread his feet to remain upright as a fight broke out across the bar. The two were secluded in a cubicle, partly obscured through the haze of smoke. His view of them was fleeting as he was bounced about by the jeering mob. The scarred-faced man looked up and was on his feet, his fists rounding as he waded into the crush. The woman seemed indifferent to the fact that she had been abandoned.

Unhappiness shoved to the back of his mind, he had to wonder what type of woman ate with royalty but drank with sailors, who was unperturbed by the language of dockers or a bar room scrap. Moving around the edge of the room, clutching his bottle to his chest, Felix wanted to finally put a name to the woman who'd hovered at the edges of his mind, just before sleep claimed him, ever since they'd first met.

∾

TRIXIE

"ANGELA GOT AWAY – why can't we?"

George leaned forward; eyes sharp in his solemn face. "Your sister got a head start because Stella never thought that anyone would dare go against her. Angel did you a disservice by putting her on notice."

"So, you think I should just go, abandon Lily to this strange foreigner?" Trixie hissed, vexation making her voice climb.

George reeled back, eyes darting to the crowd, ever watchful. Trixie wondered how far her voice would carry in this establishment – and if anyone was sober enough to pay attention.

George reached across the scarred table, smooth and black from years of use. "You're going to do whatever you need to do to make that sweet girl safe, Trix, but as I said, something is amiss. I've now been pushed out. For years, I was in on all the meetings, handing out cigarettes like confetti, acting the heavy whenever she needed it. I felt like I was her right-hand man. Now...?" He shrugged, apprehension twisting his marred face. "She's too secretive. Maybe you're right – maybe she is planning on using this foreign geezer to springboard her way up the ladder into a palace. If so? There's no way in hell you'll get away with leaving with Lily. She'll have all the ports tied up, main roads out of town, the lot. She has this town in her pocket – mostly thanks to the work that you–" He broke off as the fight erupted to his right. "Ah, hell," he growled and was on his feet, bounding into the writhing mass.

Trixie sighed, unsure if she'd done the right thing in asking George to help, letting him in on her plans. She reasoned that they'd need someone that they could trust to help them get to the docks, to move any property – maybe throw Stella off the trail. Hearing that he'd been shut out was a blow to the plan that had been forming in her mind.

Trixie tried not to let George's words weigh her down. She'd come here looking for one of the men that she'd used to fence some of the stuff that she's managed to syphon off from her jobs over the years. She'd been worried when George had seen her here, but it had proven impossible to lie to the man who was like a big brother to her. Her contact was nowhere to be seen and now she was in a foul mood. The heat of her anger was quickly extinguished when *he* slipped into the bench across from her. His face was mostly obscured by the dark beard - his hair was longer, curling over his collar and the cap that covered his head was pulled down. Even before he'd pressed the tip of his cap back with his thumb, she'd recognised the sharp gaze of Felix Huxley.

Her stomach did a long slow roll of longing. Her mind stuttered as she stared impotently at him. He set the bottle down next to his glass, reached across the table for hers, and filled them both. He drained his without breaking eye contact. She fought for equilibrium so that by the time he'd refilled his glass, she was outwardly calmer, even as her blood thrummed with awareness of him.

"How do you do that?" He held the glass between his fingers, twirled it daintily, looking at her.

"Do what?" She husked.

"Pull that mask of yours back on so effectively. It makes you hard to read. Lucky for you, I'm the observant sort."

Felix Huxley. Back in town. She wondered what he was doing here - if he was making a deal or just passing through. Her mind whirled with possibilities.

"I don't know what you mean."

His grin was unapologetic. "Sure, you do. You know," he grimaced at the taste of his drink, paused before he emptied the tumbler again. "You never did tell me your name. And I don't believe it's Mary Jones, although that was the name you gave on the guest list of the dinner party we were at together."

"We weren't together," she took her drink to avoid his intense stare, drained the contents. He'd been checking on her, just as she had with him. The knowledge gave her a perverse kick.

"Are you going to tell me your name, at least?"

She pushed her glass towards him and smiled. "Thanks for the drink."

When she rose to her feet, he clamped a hand around her wrist and she froze, her eyes flying to meet his. Her skin heated with his contact and her thoughts clouded. How could he do that when she needed her wits about her more than ever. There was a racket and a glass exploded behind her as it struck the wall. Their table rocked as a cluster of fighting bodies fell on it. Trixie yanked her hand from under them, then squeezed between the wrestling men, taking advantage of her slim build to squeeze along the wall like a rat running from a fire. For wasn't that what she was doing? Fleeing in case she got burned again. She didn't know what it was about the man; he disturbed her, and she was so unsure around him. She burst through the door and ran up the steps, out onto the streets. The damp streets shone on the milky gaslight, cabs rattled past, echoing along the dark empty streets, and disappearing into the mists. Too late, she remembered George was in the bar still, along with one of the drivers. She couldn't go back in there.

She struck out along the road, barrelling around the corner, pulling up short when she saw the two men in the shadows, elbowing off the wall that they'd been leaning against. She'd wanted to duck her head and scurry past them but could sense their intent even before they'd stepped in front of her.

"Looking to make some money, sweetheart?" The bigger man peered at her through his one eye.

His friend caught him by the shoulder. "She is all alone, John. I think the next one is free."

She lifted her hands up, stared them both right dead in the face. "I can't begin to tell you how wrong you are, on both counts. I promise you that you'll regret touching me. Just go ahead on your merry way and we'll say nothing more on the matter."

John's lips peeled back, yellow teeth flashing as he lunged for her.

∼

FELIX

USUALLY, his size was a help. Tonight, having broad shoulders meant that he couldn't slip through the crowd as easily as she had done. But he did have brute size on his side, so he ended up shoving drunken sailors and buffoons to the side with his free hand.

By the time he'd reached the street, there was no sign of her. He sighed, took a swig from his bottle as he tried to decide which way she'd head. He knew nothing about her, had no idea which way she would go. He swung right, away from the river and back into town. He dismissed the senseless decision to try and follow her. For the first time since he'd found Andrew's body on the floor of their hotel room, he felt alive. He walked around the corner and, at first, he wasn't sure what he was looking at. The fog had rolled in, so the light was murky, but he heard the shout. Heard the sickening thud of flesh striking flesh. Instinctively, he knocked the end of his bottle against the wall and started to run, brandishing the broken glass. It was her scream that made him lengthen his stride.

He stalled in the road as one man, followed the other, both bellowed in pain. She whirled on his stuttering footsteps, with her knife brandished and lethal fire blazing in her face. Blood trickled from her nostril and the corner of her mouth as her breath heaved.

He dropped the bottle in surrender, palms out. "You're fine, Mary. You're okay."

She dragged a hand across her mouth, could see the blood that stained her skin in the light, and bellowed her rage. Her hand went to the bodice of her dress that was gaping and she aimed a kick right in the gut of the one-eyed man.

Carriages rocketed past the mouth of the road, and it

seemed to draw her back to the moment. She looked at him, her swollen lower lip disappearing between her teeth. She expertly flipped the knife, presented him with the handle as she seemed to wilt in front of him.

Felix took the knife in one hand and caught her in the other before she hit the floor. "Let's get you out of here."

He sheathed the knife and slipped an arm about her slender waist, trying not to rejoice as she leaned heavily against his body. She fit perfectly under his arm as he led her down the road. One glance behind him showed one of her attackers slowly climbing to his feet. Felix paused before he slipped an arm behind her legs and swung her up into his arms, hailing one of the carriages.

One stopped almost immediately, and the driver hopped down, not at all bothered by the man with a semi-conscious woman in his arms as he opened the carriage door and kicked the step down. "Where to, sir?"

"Langham Hotel," Felix handed her into the cab and frowned as the driver coughed. His wizened gaze swung between the scruffy man and the bloodied woman asking to go to an expensive hotel.

Felix growled his exasperation, pulled a half-sovereign from his pocket, and nearly flipped it through the air. "Langham hotel," he repeated to the driver and then pulled himself into the interior.

The young woman was huddled in the corner, as white as a sheet and quivering. Felix leaned back out of the opening as he realised that he had the chance to get to spend a little time with the mysterious woman, and he used his body to shield her from the driver's curious gaze.

"And take your time," he told him before closing the door and drawing the curtain.

∼

TRIXIE

TRIXIE SENT him a look of gratitude when he settled his coat across her shoulders. Instantly, the latent warmth from his body began to ease the tremors that shuddered through her, and she gave him a small smile.

"Thank you," she said as she pulled the material around her. He was watching her in that intense way of his. This time though, she held the look. "Why were you following me?"

"It was more by luck than design that I turned right when coming out of the pub. I'd give you fair warning about frequenting those types of business, especially considering what you've just been through, but you can handle yourself – more than, I'd say. Here," he slid her knife from his belt, wiped the blood from the blade on his handkerchief, then held the knife out to her.

Mortification burned through her. She'd never had cause to use her knife, and even though they'd deserved it, she was still horrified at the rage that had burned through her. She reached out and snatched it from him, lowering her gaze. "What if there were any witnesses? You're now implicated in a crime, Mr. Huxley."

"It wouldn't be the first time... *Mary*," he drawled the

name deliberately though when she lifted her eyes to meet his cool grey one once more, humour glinted there. "And it wouldn't be too much of a stretch of the imagination to guess it's not your first one, either. Which makes a curious man such as me wonder why a lady who appears at home brushing shoulders with royalty during an extravagant dinner party was even in a docker's watering hole in the first place. You are an enigma that has given me more than enough pause for thought since the night we met. So much so that I even told my uncle of you the day before he…"

She saw his throat working as he cut the words off. Briefly, a shadow passed over his face and she could easily recall his expression when he'd been walking behind his uncle's body and her heart squeezed in sympathy. "I was sorry to hear of your uncle's passing," As soon as the words were out, she wanted to ram them back in her mouth, especially as his eyes sharpened on her.

Speculation crossed his face, and he folded his arms as he watched her. "It seems you have me at a disadvantage here, Mary. You know much about me when I know only that you can handle yourself in a street fight and that you are good at hiding your true self."

Trixie wanted to fidget under his gaze. Maybe she should tell him who she really was – it had certainly sent Morgan running for the hills. If she could get rid of him, it would leave her to clear her mind and focus on the job at hand. Until she remembered that he might just be the job she needed to facilitate her and Lily's escape.

"My name isn't Mary," she murmured, deciding to give

him a little information. "It's Beatrix." It felt alien to have her name on her lips. He was right, she was afraid to reveal her true self. How much more about her could he deduce if she remained in his company? Morbid curiosity overrode common sense and she found herself extending a hand to him in greeting. "But most people call me Trixie."

CHAPTER 16

$\mathscr{T}$rixie

"WELL, THAT LOOKED COSY,"

Trixie squeaked and whirled on George as he slunk out of the shadows. Felix's cab clattered away along the street and Trixie's mind had been occupied with the odd sense of feeling bereft now that he'd left her alone. She'd been so involved in her thoughts she'd not even noticed George waiting for her. She pulled Felix's coat closer to around her throat. "What are you doing here?"

"Were you the one that stuck it to those two morons, the ones who had a bloody nose each? I found them outside the Nag's Head, bemoaning the fact that a devil woman had stabbed one of them,"

Trixie reached inside her skirt for the large key to the

front door. "I warned them not to touch me. What are you doing here, George?"

He turned her back to face him before she could open her front door. "Checking on you," he held her chin between his forefinger and thumb, his scarred face searching hers. "They do this to you?"

"Of course."

"And it just so happened that Felix Huxley was there to fetch you home?"

"Yes, Papa," Trixie muttered and pulled her face from his hold. "He got me out of there in case the peelers came looking for me."

"He's a target for the business. You know that Stella wants him. Is it wise to be letting him touch you the way he was doing?"

Trixie sighed her exasperation. He was only voicing her treacherous thoughts, but it burned her to have them spoken aloud by the one person she loved after Lily. "He was a gentleman. We rode around the city for a bit. He told me a little about himself." *He's a fascinating man and I didn't want the night to end.*

George narrowed his one good eye and she briefly wondered if he could see those last words in her face. "Did you tell him about you?"

"My name – not my full name," she held up a hand before he could protest. "I'm not an idiot. And I remember what happened the last time I told a man the truth about myself. So, don't worry, George, the secret of the Queen of Thieves is still safe."

～

"FELIX HUXLEY IS IN TOWN AGAIN!"

Trixie felt herself stiffen as the words came tumbling out of Maisie's mouth. She'd been trying to think of a way to engineer her way round to the subject of the diamond dealer being without revealing that she'd been alone in a cab with him last night when Maisie's cry cut across the conversation she'd been having. Oblivious, Maisie continued into the room and flopped into the armchair with an exaggerated sigh. Trixie met George's gaze over the rim of her cup where he loitered against the backdrop of the tall window.

Stella's cigarette paused halfway to her lips. "I've not heard anything. Are you certain?"

Maisie's hand snatched a cake off the plate on the table, and she peeled the paper from around the sponge, shrugging as she sucked the sugar icing off her thumb. Trixie settled her teacup into its saucer. No one seemed to find the incongruity of Stella's penchant for discussing their business of criminal activity over afternoon tea and cakes as amusing as Trixie did. "Of course. The porter from the Langham saw him arrive yesterday,"

"Any news on how long he'll be in town?"

"How is *he* going to know that?" Maisie spoke around the lump of cake in her mouth. "I did find out from someone else that Felix told the manager that he was in town on business and would hopefully only need his room a week, though would let him know if he needed it any longer. Paid in cash, as always. Big wad of notes,"

Maisie waggled her brows. "He went out late last night and returned in the very early hours of this morning, alone I may add. He asked for a barber to be sent to his room this morning, and that's all I know so far. I've asked the porter to keep his ear out, see if he's been invited out to any dinner events. Maybe our Trixie here can pay him a visit, get him to make his love-eyes at her again."

She happened to know that Felix was in town to settle Andrew Huxley's estate. The skin on the back of her hand still tingled where Felix had pressed his lips to it as he'd dropped her off last night. She'd been careful not to reveal too much about herself but couldn't get the man off her mind. She was conflicted. He was a bit of an enigma himself – he spoke of travel and far-off places, and he'd broken a bottle to use as a weapon in a street fight, without a second thought.

"I'm sure your gossip network has the whole city sealed off in one way or another, Maisie," Trixie laughed.

"What happened to your face?" The half-devoured cake was on the precipice of Maisie's open mouth as the other girl stared at the bruises.

"Tripped on the rug in my room," Trixie intoned. "Trying to use the chamber pot without lighting the lamp,"

"Foozler," Maisie giggled as she popped the cake into her mouth.

Trixie dipped her head at the insult. Better they thought her an idiot than wonder what she was doing out at the docks and fighting off would-be rapists. "We were just talking about New York," she informed Maisie, "though now you're here, we can find out where we're up to with jobs on the home soil."

Maisie nodded and used her sleeve to wipe her mouth when Stella interrupted her. "Wait. Having Felix Huxley back in town changes everything."

"My passage to America is booked though?" Trixie sighed, even though this was exactly what she'd hoped the news of Felix's presence in town would bring. She hadn't known how to let the other woman know and could have kissed Maisie for her timing.

"I want to know why he's here."

"You wanted me gone to take the heat off you?" Trixie knew she was playing devil's advocate.

Stella jabbed her cigarette towards Trixie, a determined set to her chin. "His deals are legendary; his suppliers are the best in the business."

Trixie put the cup on the table. "He also deals with people who are loaded and therefore have the best security. Getting past him, considering how fast he passes the stones off, will make it a tough job to pull off."

"Huge unset stones that will be a doddle to flog," Stella continued her musing. "This could be the final job to set me up for life."

Trixie paused and blinked at her boss as hope made her heart lurch in her chest. "Your final job? Would that mean that it would be my final job, too?"

Stella's dark laugh was husky. "Maisie is right, you are a foozler. No, you're too good to let go."

～

Felix

"Here I was, wracking my brains on how I could find you and you find me instead though, with what limited knowledge I have about you, I feel that this is an engineered meeting rather than one of chance." Felix smiled, watching as she dismissed the man with the scarred face with a single nod. "May I?" He tapped the back of the chair, pulled it out to take his seat, and ordered a whisky drink from a passing waiter that rushed through the hotel restaurant.

"That's an expensive whisky," Trixie said, and he smiled, pleased that she knew the difference.

Felix noted that the glowering man remained where he had sight of Trixie still. "Friend of yours?"

Trixie glanced to where George watched them. "More like family,"

Felix leaned back as the waiter returned with his glass and set it down, waited until they were alone. He took his time looking at her, ravenous with longing. This time, she let him look, a small smile playing about her full lips. She'd dressed to suit the clientele of an upmarket hotel and looked perfectly matched to be waiting in a hotel lobby, maybe for a lover. That she was there for him gave him a sense of proprietory over her that he had no right to feel. She was still a stranger, careful and measured around him. There was a slight discolouration to the side of her mouth, that she'd tried to cover with make-up. "How are you after the other night? How did you know where to find me?"

"I'm fine," she toyed with the gin glass in front of her, "and I remembered you gave the driver this address. It was simply a case of waiting until you came back,"

Felix sipped at the whisky, enjoying the heat from the liquid. "Why do I get the feeling that you know what room I'm staying in, too?"

The little flicker of glory in her face lit his blood. Why her? He'd met so many beautiful women over the years, why this one who was secretive and who puzzled him? Maybe that was why. His inquisitive nature loved to discover how things worked. Wasn't that what Andrew had said made him a great entrepreneur?

"How long are you in town for?"

"Ah," he bobbed his brows, "finally something that she doesn't know for certain. I told you that I must finalise Andrew's estate. I'm hoping that it won't take more than a week. I have a little bit of business to do then I might head back to…" he sent her a rueful smile. "In all honesty, I don't know where I am to go next. This country holds a lot of precious memories for me, but also much heartache."

"For your uncle?"

He nodded, a frown pulling on his brows, unsure why he felt the need to offload his thoughts with her. "Yes, and the man who raised me."

"You weren't raised by your family?"

"Mother died a few days after I was born, my father passed away in the dead of winter when I was six. Father

Frank Huxley took me in to save me from the work-house," Memory turned the grey of his eyes stormy as he stared into the glass. "I found Frank in his bed one morning – he'd died in his sleep. For a while, I did end up in the workhouse, until Andrew found out. He travelled the globe to get me out of there."

"He wasn't your uncle?"

He lifted his stormy eyes to hers, slid his eyes to George. "You don't have to be blood to call a person family. In the end, it was easier to call Andrew an uncle than to have to explain the tenuous link every time we met someone new. It seems the people that I do business with prefer a person to have a conventional background that they can relate to. It inspires trust. Besides, he and his brother gave me a life, taught me everything that I know. They are the reason why I am alive, and not begging in the streets or scraping a wage out of the gutter at the docks."

"His passing must have been difficult for you,"

Felix drained the glass to give him time to ensure that the words wouldn't get stuck in his throat. He cleared it, just to make sure. "The worst, especially as I had no warning. Just like Frank, he just… went. He had so much vitality left…. I miss him,"

When her finger stroked the back of his hand, it snapped his mind from melancholy to awakening that had his breath leaving him in a rush. She pulled her hand back quickly, her cheeks turning pink under the powder, almost as if she'd forgotten that they were in a public space under the baleful glare of her watchman.

"You're easy to talk to," he admitted, "which is surprising considering I know next to nothing about you and here I am confessing things that have been keeping my mind company for months. How do you do that?"

"Practice," she smiled.

He found himself longing to know much about her and searched his mind for ways to dig into her psyche a bit further. "Do you have family, any proper blood relatives?"

He could see the indecision in her face as she looked at him before she nodded. "A little sister,"

Her lower lip disappeared between her teeth, and he knew that that was all she was going to say on the subject.

"Are you busy tonight? I was wondering if you would care to accompany me as my guest to an event? A small dinner for the arts, not as grand as dining with royalty but... it means that I can spend a little more of my time not getting to know you and you can continue avoiding my questions."

CHAPTER 17

*T*rixie

"I WAS WONDERING when you'd wear the tanzanite again," he murmured into her ear. Having him so close to her sent gooseflesh racing across her skin and the thrum of her blood in her ears drowned out the conversation around them. She wasn't sure how he managed it by just being himself. She dropped her gaze to his mouth and wondered how shocked he would be if she leaned in and brushed her lips to his as she had fantasized about doing so often in the past month.

She'd been with him every day in the last month and her life had felt almost... normal, even though she spent her daylight hours with Stella, negotiating the delicate balance of giving her boss enough information to keep her interested without giving away Felix's secrets. She'd had to come up with excuses to leave Felix early some nights to go and break into houses, and crack a safe or two, if only to keep Stella happy. Every time Stella asked a question about Felix, she'd had to come up with more elaborate reasons about why Felix hadn't yet left, why he hadn't had a delivery, why she hadn't yet made her move, why, why, why…

For that was how she felt. She wanted to protect him. She was wrapped up, consumed with thoughts of the diamond dealer, his laughter, his stories… She knew that she had fallen in love with him. She loved to simply watch him; his beautiful eyes, his kind smile, his amiable nature. He seemed to be everything that she had dreamed of in a man. He was decent, compassionate, honourable. The people he dealt with treated him with deference even when he shimmied along the lines of the law in his business. She tried to remain in the background, not wanting to be noticed but he'd involve her in the conversation and would seek her opinion on subjects.

Every night he left her at the door with a chaste goodbye, and every night she hoped that he would kiss her, just once. Instead, he simply gave her a neat bow and clambered back into the carriage, waiting until she'd let herself into her building. And each night, George had met her in the doorway to tease her about keeping the man panting for more, when it was the other way around.

Felix had treated her cordially, with respect afforded to a woman of better standing, certainly more than she truly deserved.

Her hand went to the pendant around her neck. Of

course, he'd recognise the rare gem that had been too beautiful to liquidate. Instead, she had palmed it and had it made into a necklace.

"Where did you get it?" he dipped his head so that his cheek grazed her hair when he leaned in closer and she nearly swooned. "And if you tell me a man gave it to his paramour, I shall hate it forever."

She giggled, thrilled that he sounded jealous. It was the only sign he'd shown her that he was interested in her. "I earned it."

His eyes moved between hers, their grey warm and liquid. "Is there a man – one that I should be aware of?"

Her mouth parted in shock. "Why... we've been together every night this week, Felix, and for most nights in the last month. Why would you think such a thing?"

"I'm not a fool, Trixie," the sound of her name on his lips trickled over her like molten gold. "I know that I have told you much of my life whilst you've given me not even the bare bones of yours. My business here is almost done. I have one large shipment in my possession, another due and..." he swallowed, "I find myself considering my future. Before I arrived in London, I was only moving from one moment to the next. For the first time in my life, I want to remain in one place, if it means I can stay with you."

"Felix Huxley!" The booming voice blasted through the thrall that Felix's word had her in, and Trixie had to fight to find her equilibrium. She moved back from him slightly as Felix looked to the gentleman whose voice had interrupted their low exchange. "I thought that was you, old chap. I hear that you have a shipment that's just hit our shores today? Did I hear that right?"

Felix spun on a heel, angling away from Trixie. "That's true, Captain. And I hear that you know a man who's interested in that shipment."

"Well, if it's the same quality as the one you sold to my man in York, then I may know of several dealers. Just how big a delivery are we talking?"

"Excuse me a moment, my dear," Felix nodded to Trixie, sending her a wink. "Let's step over here, Captain, away from delicate ears."

Disappointment flooded her, her eyes burning with unshed tears as realisation blasted her. The large shipment that Stella had been waiting on was here. That meant two things. Her time with Felix was coming to an end. Felix would take possession of the stones in the next day or so – all she had to do was follow the delivery. There would be enough in there where she could take half for herself and then arrange an escape for her and Lily. But her pain wasn't from the terror of breaking away from Stella, or the dangers that would come with fleeing the queen of thieves. It came from the aching knowledge that she was going to have to rob off a man who'd stolen her heart.

∼

TRIXIE

. . .

"TRIX,"

Trixie turned to the low muttering of her name, her hand on the opening of the carriage with Felix's hand in the small of her back. All evening, she had been preoccupied with thoughts of leaving. She wasn't sure how she was going to let Felix know that she couldn't even think of a future with him. He'd concluded his business and they were leaving the grand-looking town house when she'd heard the quiet voice.

George remained in the shadows along the street, though she recognised his familiar shape. She excused herself from Felix, pressing a hand to his chest when he tried to follow her.

"What's wrong?" she hissed when she reached him, disturbed by George's anguished expression, and his words turned her blood to stone.

"It's bad," George whispered, "It's Lily. She's in danger. I've been sent to get you. She needs you, Trix."

CHAPTER 18

Trixie

TRIXIE BURST in through the front door, her heels echoing with George's across the bare floor of the warehouse as she rounded the stairs. Memories of when she'd first arrived there swirled in her mind, causing her to fight for clarity. *Lily.*

She raced up the staircase, fury licking through her, and she crashed through the office door. There, in the middle of the room, Lily sat on one of the chairs. Her face was bloodied, and she had a fresh cut above her eye; blood trickled down her cheek and pooled on her dress. Her eyes were bloodshot from crying. But it was the terror in her eyes that was nearly Trixie's undoing. Instead of exploding, she was instantly calm as she dragged her gaze from her sister to Stella, who was lounging in her highbacked chair, her feet stacked one atop of the other on her desk.

"Ah, the errant wanderer returns. I knew that George would be the one to go straight to you – funny how he always knows these things, isn't it? You can go, George – but don't go far. We have unfinished business,"

Trixie didn't take her eyes off her boss. She had seen her like this only once before – the fanatic light in her eyes, the cruel lash of her voice – in Manchester. She couldn't look at Lily, tried to block out her soft sobs that had started as soon as Trixie had rushed in.

"But, boss, I ain't..."

"Out!" Stella screeched, her ice mask slipping for an instant. "That's better, just us girls," Her sing-song voice was back in place as George closed the door.

"Why is my sister all battered, Stella? Just what the hell is going on?"

Stella's boots struck the floor as she straightened up, the sound ricocheting in the room, and she curled her lip. "You White girls – you're all the same! Lying, conniving little snakes! I should have put a bullet in you both myself, after what Angel did to me. And I will do, once I've got what I need from you!"

Trixie looked at Lily, caught the slight shake of her head. "I don't... who did that to her?"

"I did! When I found that little hedge-creeper in my room, going through my private correspondence. She reliably informs me that I had it all wrong," she spread her hands, sarcasm dripping from her voice. "That she won't marry the prince that I've chosen for her. That I have wasted my time all these years investing in her, coaching her. Then I find this, secreted under her mattress!" She snatched the letters off her desk, flung them into Trixie's face. Trixie took the papers, saw the familiar scrawl of Lily's on the papers – a letter. *A love letter! Oh, Lily, you crazy fool. We were almost there.* "She loves a draper's son – a worthless street rat, just like she is. Well, she can't marry a dead man, can she?"

Lily emitted a wail, full of pain that twisted Trixie's insides. "You had a man killed?"

"You bet I did! No one makes a fool out of me – no one!" Stella pressed to her feet, leaned over her desk as she glared at Trixie. "And then, after I slapped her about a bit, I get her to tell me why you've been acting so secretive, so withdrawn from the business of late. You think you can pull the same stunt you did in Manchester? You want out?"

"No, I–"

"Don't you lie to me!" Stella's face contorted in rage, spittle erupting from her stained lips. "Go and get me those diamonds off that imbecile you've been lusting over. I've seen for myself how you are around him." Trixie reared back and Stella cackled. "That's right, you didn't see me watching, always watching. I *want* those diamonds – and don't you think about skimming anything off the top of them, either. See? I know that's what you've been doing – how else would you get that fancy trinket around your neck? You won't get out of this country, either of you. I have men watching every dock in this land, and I have a photograph of you heading to every newspaper.

Let's see how far the queen of thieves gets when the coppers know what you look like! You have until sundown tomorrow. You bring me those stones, and then I might consider letting *her* live long enough to earn me some coin in one of my brothels."

"Stella, please, don't hurt her – she's just a child!"

"You are not the one in control here – you never have been, Beatrix. I put Angel into a hole in the ground, I can do it with you, too! That boyfriend of yours, too, if you don't give me what I want."

Trixie's stare turned to stone. "Angela is dead?" For all these years, she'd hoped and prayed that her sister had escaped the clutches of this madwoman. "Why tell me now?"

"Because I no longer need anything from you – if I'd have told you that I caught that wretch and put her in the ground, you would have been less than cooperative for me over the years. So, I hedged my bets." Stella sniffed; her tone nonchalant, as she sat back down.

Trixie shouldn't have been surprised that Stella would talk about murder so casually. "Where is my sister buried?"

Stella lit a cigarette with a shaking hand, the only remaining outward sign of her fury. She inhaled, hung onto the smoke for a moment, the words that came out of her mouth wrapped in smoke, "You go get me those stones."

≈

FELIX

FELIX LEANED his head back against the wood of the door, and sighed, his warm breath ghosting in front of his face into the cold night air. She either wasn't home or was ignoring her door, so he'd simply wait it out. She had to come home – or leave – at some point. She couldn't just vanish on him and not say goodbye. He shoved away the feeling of foreboding, unable to process anything other than her not being safe. She'd not even bid him good-night. Whatever George had said to her had been enough to take her away from him without a backwards glance. He'd seen the look of utter terror on her face as she ran past him with George earlier that evening.

"You're wasting your time," the voice was low, so low that Felix wondered first where it was coming from until the shadows to his right shifted and took the form of a man. *George.* "She's not here."

Felix leaned forward, hope flowing through him. "She can't be far away – you're like her shadow, George. Where did you take her?"

"Not anymore," George said dully, tugging down the peak of his cap. "Do yourself a favour. Get out of the country – today. Go."

Felix stood up, panic closing in on him, which sent his voice climbing, "Please, George. I need to see her. Tell me where you took her."

George juggled the large black sack slung over his shoulder to settle it more comfortably on his back. "She's not who you thought she was. I know that she would want you to be safe though. You're the only one who ever made her smile, Huxley. Take comfort in that, man – God knows there aren't many things to be happy about in this life."

Felix followed him around the side of the building, tried to call him back, only he was shouting into thin air. George had disappeared.

~

FELIX LET himself into his hotel room, waited for the sconces to be illuminated by the young man who'd seen him to his room. When he was alone, he shucked off his overcoat before he speared his fingers through his dark hair as thoughts tumbled through his mind. *Where is she?*

She needed his help; he knew that much but also knew that she'd never revealed anything of substance about herself – not even her last name. At the time, he'd been happy that she'd shown him an element of trust. Now, he cursed himself for all the trusting fools under the sun. He'd lost his heart to a complete stranger, and now he had no way of knowing where she was. He scrubbed his hands down his face, trying to get a grip on his scattered thoughts.

Somebody must know something. In the morning, he would go through Andrew's book. Andrew had made the nefarious contacts – Felix had kept the exchanges relatively legal, skirting the edges of the law. Maybe the book would help him.

He crossed to the bureau and poured himself a brandy, gulped it down, and waited for the blaze in his throat to ease the ache in his belly. Why hadn't he pressed her for more information? Why had she held so much of herself back from him? Urgency weighed in and he walked into the bedroom, intent on searching for Andrew's book when he saw the painting on the bed. His eyes darted to the safe stowed away in the wall, the door was wide open. He knew even before he checked that it was empty.

∾

TRIXIE

TRIXIE TOSSED the large velvet pouch onto the desk. It made a satisfying clatter as it skidded to a halt next to Stella's ashtray. "Here," she barked, "You've got what you wanted. Now, you can let us go."

Stella picked up the bag, tugging on the strings that had secured the edges together. "In case you need reminding, you are not in charge. You don't tell me what to do, Trixie White. You don't ever tell me what to do." She pulled her desk blotter across the wood towards her and upended the pouch, making a small, satisfied gasp as the precious gemstones skidded out across the surface of the desk. Deep green emeralds and blood reds of rubies shone in the light from her desk. "I was right!" Stella crowed. "Look at these beauties – they're gonna make me a pretty penny!"

"See? You've checked them; I held up my end of the deal."

"I checked because I don't trust you as far as I could throw you. You only did what I wanted you to because I had your precious sister."

"Of course, I did – look at what you did to her. All she did was fall in love," Trixie couldn't help the tears that sprung into her eyes.

"All she did was *betray* me – the same as Angel, the same as you. I gave you everything, I treated her like she was mine." Stella snapped, her flat palm slapping the desk. 'I had plans – and you both ruined them."

Fear drove Trixie on as Lily whimpered behind her. "You don't have to put us in the ground, Stella. We can work. You know I can turn my hand to anything."

"Enough!" She patted the air in front of her, taking her sweet time closely examining the stones, turning them in the light, before slipping them into the pouch. She tied the two strings in a knot, dangled the bag from the tip of her finger as she pursed her lips in consideration of Trixie. "You know, I have enough on my plate tonight. I can't trust a single one of you – my boys are out looking for that idiot George. Seems I tipped him off that I wanted his head on a spike because I was so furious with you," She set the bag on her desk, and linked her fingers, resting her chin on her hands.

Trixie rushed around the edge of the desk, dropping to her knees, and laying her head in Stella's lap, sending the boss skittering backwards.

"Please, Stella, don't hurt us. I'm sorry, I should never have betrayed you!"

She made a sound of disgust and made a waving motion with her hands. 'Put them in the cellar,' The two men who'd been standing guard on either side of her stepped forward.

Trixie fought them, struggled against the restraints that she felt tightening around her wrists. "Wait!" She tried to get purchase on the floor as she was dragged across it. Lily's distressed sounds pressed against the gag as she was hauled upwards and towards the door. Trixie opened her mouth to defend her sister, but the cries were cut off when the hand clapped over her mouth.

～

TRIXIE

"YOU SHOULD HAVE RUN when you had the chance," Lily's dull voice echoed off the stone walls. She'd made her bleeding face worse by scraping her skin against the rock-filled wall to pull the gag down before she'd finally lay on her side. "I wouldn't have blamed you. I should have been more careful. Robert is dead because of me. Now... She's going to kill us, and it's all my fault."

Trixie could hear the scattering of rats, as they made their way along the wall of the cellar. Somewhere in the dank room, water dripped like the rhythmic ticking of a grandfather clock. Dawn light had edged slowly back the darkness so that she could see her sister slumped over in the corner. She'd been still and quiet for so long, Trixie had assumed that she'd fallen asleep.

"I made you a promise once that I wouldn't ever leave you. Of course, I came back. All you did was fall in love, Lily – you didn't kill him. Love makes us do funny things." Stormy grey eyes moved through her mind's eye, making her own sting with unshed tears. *I didn't even get to say goodbye.*

"But now you're here with me, trapped," the last word was whispered.

Despair pressed in on her. She had no way of knowing how they were going to get out of this, she just knew that their life depended on her being able to think of a way out of it. She hoped that George had done as she'd asked and ran. She hoped that Felix would forgive her for what she'd done. Her arms burned from being tied behind her; she shifted, trying to find a reprieve from the stress position.

There, through the gloom, the dull brass ring caught her eye. She rolled onto her knees and shuffled forwards towards it, trying to work out what she was looking at.

"Lily!" she hissed, "Look! Is that...?" When she recognised it, hope pushed against dejection, and she was suddenly spurned into action.

CHAPTER 19

❦

*F*elix

NOT EVEN THE cold water he'd splashed on his face could ease the gritty eyes from lack of sleep. One glance in the looking glass told him that he looked as bedraggled as he felt. He'd spent the night with the hotel manager, having ripped into him over the lack of security, even though deep down he'd been more furious with himself for not having his normal foresight to put the delivery in the hotel's safe like he normally did. Despite reassurances that the room safes in the hotel were the best money could buy, someone had still managed to get into his room and steal his property. He was usually so fastidious, and Andrew had always hammered it home over the years on what he should do to protect the investment. Now it was gone, vanished into thin air.

Or at least he thought it had been thin air before the hotel had had a complimentary breakfast delivered to his rooms, complete with a copy of this morning's newspaper.

His toast was stone cold, his coffee congealing, as he stared again at the grainy image on the front page. Her secrecy now made sense to him, why she'd always set herself apart from the room, and was the most observant person he'd ever known. She'd known gemstones – almost as much as he did. Now, as he stared at the familiar face of an artist's rendition of what Trixie looked like, fury boiled inside.

He knew who had his stones. He knew who'd broken into his room and who had broken his trust. He'd been used by the queen of thieves herself.

~

STELLA

"THANKS FOR COMING – with two of them, I didn't want to attempt to apprehend them any further," Stella sent the policeman a sultry smile that deepened when his cheeks turned to scarlet under her knowing gaze.

"That's my job, Miss Stella,"

The older one of the two wasn't as fazed by her and his voice was curt, "You sure it's the girl in the paper? The one they captioned 'The Queen of Thieves'?"

Stella stopped by the door and waited for one of them

to open it for her before she led the way down the steps. "Oh, I'm quite certain, though she had another younger girl with her. Had to have two of my employees help me restrain them. Couldn't believe that I caught them in my office, red-handed!"

"Any idea what they were looking for? I mean, she mostly steals jewellery, and you said you mostly deal in fabric, madam."

Stella surreptitiously patted the hidden pocket in her skirts, full of the gemstones that Trixie had stolen for her, hiding her glee through a shrug. The sound of their descent echoed in the long hall, the gaslight lamp she held aloft making their shadows dance crudely along the jagged walls.

"I'm not sure what they thought they would find. Luckily, I was working late and heard them. Normally, I would have been at home getting my beauty sleep,"

"I'm not so sure that you'd need that, Miss Stella." The young policeman muttered and Stella sent another demure look back at him.

This time, she heard the light tap administered to his arm by the older copper. "We've been after her for quite some time – always been one step ahead of us, until now. We thought we'd had a breakthrough yesterday when we had the image delivered anonymously. Bit of a coincidence that she happened to break into your place last night, wouldn't you say?"

Stella's eye glinted when she drew to a halt outside of the cellar doors, her lips curving dangerously though her voice was sickly sweet. "I hadn't seen the paper when I caught them last night – there was no one in the police station when I sent one of my boys to get you." The heavy-set key clunked into the lock and squeaked as she turned it. "Besides, regardless of what you've heard about me, I like to do my bit to help rid the country of this criminal scum."

She hauled on the door and stepped through the opening, holding the lamp aloft as she gestured that they follow her. The light swung wildly left, then right. Quickly, she took more steps into the centre of the room, pivoting in a complete circle to survey the space. Rope was coiled in a pile, one of the cords trailing off. Stella tracked it, her heart dropping into her stomach when she saw the small hatch door in the floor that was wide open. She rushed to it and peered down into the empty sewer below.

CHAPTER 20

*F*elix

Y*OU'RE the only one who ever made her smile.*

George's words kept bubbling up inside, frothing about inside with his feelings of hurt, and betrayal. Felix's fingers drummed a staccato beat on the newspaper photograph. He kept coming back to the same question: *why?* Why had she gotten to know him? Was she that much of a trickster? The feelings that he'd had for her had been real – *were* real. She'd not confessed to having feelings for him – if she had meant to lead him on a merry dance, surely, she could have played it differently to get close to him. She could have taken the other stones – simply broken in the night he'd told her they'd been delivered.

Unanswered questions led to more, leading him

around in endless circles. Nothing made sense. Why had she allowed him into her secluded life, told him her real name? Although she hadn't given him much more to go on. Instead, he'd been the one to chase her. According to the paper, she had a long and illustrious career behind her. Why had her picture been printed the day after she'd fled? George had been at her place...

The sack on his back! Felix closed his eyes, recalling the gruff man, how he'd fidgeted, how he'd warned him to run. Had he been the one to break in and she'd taken the blame? George was a bruiser – he'd waded into a bar fight. To break into a hotel without being noticed took finesse and skill.... Attributes that he could see Trixie having, not George. Felix growled as he shoved to his feet. He just couldn't let all these questions go unanswered. It would drive him insane.

The newspaper didn't say anything about her location – just a city-wide call to warn its people of the blight on society. Felix grabbed his coat and rushed to the door of his suite. He knew where she resided, maybe he could see more in the daylight. Maybe he could ask around the pub at the docks. Someone had to know something.

He snatched open the door, then froze as he stared at the familiar-looking hotel maid who was stood in the doorway.

~

STELLA

. . .

THE DOOR BOOMED BACK into its frame as Stella stomped across the floor, vibrating with anger. She came to a stop near her desk, hands on her hips and she closed her eyes as she tried to get her temper back under control. Having the peelers' mocking laughter still ringing in her ears did nothing to soothe her fury.

How had they got out of their bindings? Stella pinched the bridge of her nose and knew that the mistake had been not leaving them where she could see them. In her mind, it looked more genuine to have put them in the cellar when the police arrived. She should have tied them up herself – though why hadn't she thought to use metal cuffs to hold them?

"That girl always had a knack of getting out of scrapes," she muttered to the empty room. At some point over the years, she must have learned how to get out of a knot. She hadn't even contemplated that hatch in the corner. Not to worry, she sighed, she'd set the police on the girls' trail, and she had the docks and ports all on alert in case they tried to buy tickets. It was just a shame as she'd intended on rescuing Lily and bundling the girl off to her Russian suitor for a decent price, rather than having the deal go down the toilet with nothing to show for her efforts over the years. She sighed again, patting her hair as she felt her temper slipping down to a simmer. She smoothed her hands over her skirts, then retrieved the pouch of gems from her pocket, bouncing them against her palm.

"Not a total waste of time," she muttered as she rounded the desk and took her seat. The quality of the stones and the price that they were going to fetch would certainly ease some of the burn of the betrayal. She'd have a cigarette to calm her nerves and then maybe she would choose one of the stones for herself, have it set in a pendant as Trixie had done.

As the acrid smoke slipped out between her parted lips, she turned the bag upside down, grinning as the stones tumbled across the polished surface of the desk. A smile that quickly turned to ice as she frowned and roughed the stones to make their surfaces glint in the light. Not a single one of them glittered as they had done in the earlier hours of the morning. She threw the cigarette into the ashtray as she realised that they were all clear stones. No rubies, no emeralds... *Glass.*

Stella slowly sat back, her mind whirling. She'd had them, she'd handled them, she'd kept them on her since Trixie and Lily had been taken to the cellar. The event went over and over in her mind; Trixie coming in, Trixie begging... Stella pressed her fingers to her mouth, her heart thudding dully.

Trixie had fallen on her, begging her to spare their lives, pulling everyone's attention from her hands. She'd used the classic distraction to switch the bag.

Stella screamed, swiping a forearm across her desk, sending the worthless cut-glass stones tumbling across her office floor.

∼

FELIX

. . .

"I KNOW YOU, DON'T I?" Felix frowned, "the girl who fainted at the dinner party… the first night I met Trixie? That was you, wasn't it?"

Maisie lowered her hand from where she'd meant to knock on the door and had nearly hit him. Eyes darted into the room behind him, along the corridor behind her then she faced him. She gave him a brief nod. "Yes, sir."

"Then you know her!" Urgency pushed into his voice, and he reached for her, eyes pleading. "Please, tell me where she is!"

"I can't!" she pulled on her wrist, "and *you* were told to leave! Your room doesn't look like you've packed a thing!"

Shock made him drop her arm. "George – he said the same thing to me. You are all in on it?"

"I don't have time for this," Maisie reached into the pocket of her apron, "Here. She risked everything to get this back to you. And this, too." She heaped his black velvet pouch on top of a folded piece of paper. She cupped his open palm in her own and met his surprised expression with an earnest one of her own. "She is a good girl really, Felix Huxley. All the thieving… she wasn't given much of a choice in it. She did everything to save her sister, including giving up a life of her own. She wanted to say goodbye but… you get me instead. You have to know that what she wrote in the note… she meant it," Maisie patted him on the hand and then turned, hurrying back towards the door for the stairs.

"Wait, please!" Felix chased her, having to sprint to

catch her before she reached the door. "Please, you know her. You know where she is, tell me. I have to see her,"

"She's gone, Felix. She had to go, else she was going to the bottom of the Thames, or the hangman's noose after what was done to her, setting her up with the police and all."

"Wait," Felix stuffed the note into his pocket and opened his pouch. He pulled out the largest stone he could find, pushed it at Maisie. "Please, Miss. I have no interest in making things worse for her, I just... I need to see her," Felix watched the myriad of emotions ripple across the girl's face, indecision warring with loyalty. "I know just the buyer here in the city who will give you enough for that stone alone to get you away from here. Just give me the name of where she's gone."

Maisie sighed, lips firming as she opened her hand. "I don't know where she's going to. She wouldn't tell me, but I was the one who booked their travel. She used an alias – Francesca Huxley."

∼

TRIXIE

LILY'S ARM slid through hers, leaning her head on Trixie's shoulder. The spike of St. Colman's cathedral punctured the rolling green hills of Ireland, looming above Queenstown. The dark expanse of water stretched between their ship and land, between danger and escape. Gulls soared on the sea air, swooping into the churning waters of the ship's wake, and the fresh Irish breeze slapped at their faces. The deck was quieter than down below, passengers making the most of the warmth of being inside.

"Are we safe yet?"

Trixie leaned her cheek onto Lily's. "I'm not sure we ever will be. We need to keep a low profile whilst travelling still, probably even until we've got through New York. Stella will have that port covered and we must get off and away without being seen. I'm not sure that these disguises will hold up under close scrutiny."

"Might I suggest a different port to disembark from, Mrs Huxley?"

The two women turned to the voice on their right, Trixie's heart leaping into her throat. But, instead of a stern-looking official face, she was staring into the beautiful stormy grey eyes, a playful smile making his lips twitch as the wind tousled his hair across his forehead. He was leaning on the railing a little way from them, fingers loosely linked.

"Felix?" she whispered, "What are – how?" She felt Lily relax by her side when she addressed him by his name, though her blood thundered in her ears.

Felix slid his forearms along the wooden railing until he was closer to them both, his eyes roving her face like a starved man. "I got your letter."

Trixie's eyes darted behind him, around the empty deck. "I, er…" she looked back at Felix. "I don't understand how…?"

"Well," Felix rotated so that he stood sideways to the

rail, his tone conversational, "with great difficulty, Mrs Huxley. However, it turns out that the network of loyal friends whom you've helped and worked with across the years – the ones responsible for seeing you to the rowing boat to get you out of England – are also susceptible to a man grovelling on his knees, crippled with love loss, and bearing shiny diamonds."

"You bribed them?"

Felix winked, extending a hand to wave as he leaned forward conspiratorially. "I had help, Trixie – your people didn't simply give you up."

Trixie caught the movement and gasped when she saw George hovering behind Felix. He looked decidedly self-conscious in the smart black suit of a man in service.

"Have you met my new valet?" Felix grinned at her.

George tugged on his collar. "Alright, Trix. He, uh, he laid in on a bit thick like, felt sorry for him. You know," he blushed.

She rushed forward with her arms open and into her friend's embrace. "I told you to take what was left in my rooms and go. It was enough to get you started,"

George patted her back, extending a hand to Lily as he embraced her, too. "You know me, kid. Never one to follow the rules. Besides, couldn't leave him running his mouth off all around London. He woulda gotten his head in a noose before too long,"

Felix straightened up. "Thanks for the vote of confidence, George. How about you take Lily down below deck so I can speak to my good lady, here?"

George dropped a kiss on Trixie's crown and slung an arm around Lily's waist, guiding her towards the doors.

"I can't believe it. You're here," she said, wonder shining in her eyes. "I thought I'd tied everything up in a neat bow, set George up with what I had so he could get away. Maisie–"

"Maisie is currently somewhere in the north of the country, though she does plan to come back to America. She prefers the weather there. She refused to come with me after she'd connected me with George – though, with the stone she has, she'll be comfortable, Trixie."

Trixie shook her head, dumbfounded. Everything she'd meticulously planned… all different. He had no idea of the danger he'd put himself in. "Stella, she killed Lily's man and my sister. She won't stop searching, Felix. She found me once before. Oh, what have you done?"

Felix took her by the hands, threaded his fingers with hers. "She's lost the best in her team. Lots of them have gone underground because she's going demented trying to find you all. Lots of them have turned on her because she shopped you to the police. They know that she gave you up. There is honour amongst thieves, Trixie."

Her brows puckered. "How do you know this?"

"You're not the only one with a network. Now, about that letter…?" He reached inside his pocket and carefully unfolded it, turning his body to try and stop the wind from whipping it out of his hand. "You wrote here that –"

"I know what it says," she chided him gently, "I wrote the ruddy thing."

"You say that you are sorry, that spending time with

me was the happiest time of your life, that you love me," he pressed on, "that you borrowed the gems but that you had no choice. You took two of the stones to help pay for the travel and that you will pay me back as soon as you can,"

"You followed me just to get your payment?" she moved back as if slapped, hurt stinging her more than the wind at her cheeks.

Felix chuckled, folded the letter, and slid it into his pocket. "No, you misunderstand me. Look, I promise I'll get better at the smooth talk – I'm usually rather good at it, but you've always disturbed my thoughts. I blame you,"

Her lips curved, as she allowed his words to sink in. "I turn your brain to fog?"

"Every time I'm near you. It drove me insane having to leave you on the doorstep every night. In my mind, I told myself it was too soon to propose marriage. You trusted me with your name, but very little else. I know that you're the best jewel thief in the business. That you can crack any safe and have stolen from a policeman who was trying to arrest you. That you're a demon at cards. Maisie and then George told me snippets about you – but you don't share much with many people at all, do you?"

Trixie tilted her head as she contemplated him. "You know all this about me, and yet you still came to find me?"

"A man in love will do the most foolish of things," he closed the distance between them once more, this time sliding his hand around her waist. "A man in love will follow you to the ends of the earth, Beatrix White, thief of my heart."

"Felix… Do you know what you're letting yourself in for? I have no idea where I'm going, where I'll end up. How Lily and I will survive…"

"That's how I've spent the last twenty years of my life."

"What will we do for work? I left everything behind – I have nothing, other than a few quid. I don't want to steal, I never did. This is meant to be a new start. I can't be a thief anymore, Felix."

"My uncle was a wealthy man, Trixie. I've heard that my wife is a resourceful woman who can turn her hand to anything,"

She smiled as finally, she allowed herself to leap into that bubble of love, to bask in the warmth of his gaze as he watched her. She slid her hands up over his chest. "I'm only borrowing your name, you know – it was the first one that came to mind when Maisie asked me,"

"Oh, I know it's only borrowed, though I do intend to have the captain rectify that at his earliest convenience,"

"You want to marry me?"

He rested his forehead to hers, his eyes drifting closed on a breath of a sigh. "I want to hold you and never let you go again. I love you. I think I've loved you since the first moment I saw you."

Her hands linked behind his head, and she stood on tiptoes, her nose grazing his as she pressed her lips to his and sunk into the kiss. "I shouldn't be kissing you this way, sir," she leaned back, her mouth moist from his kiss. "I'm a married woman,"

Felix laughed, dipped his head once more to hers, wondering if he would ever have his fill of this beautiful creature and all her many facets, like the most stunning diamond he'd ever looked upon.

She dragged her mouth from his when the door banged open and a couple spilled out onto the deck, walking away from the entwined couple. Trixie leaned her head on his shoulder, her eyes on the horizon, the stark sky darkening as night approached. Dare she hope that they had made it? She'd been prepared to walk away from him, had tried to get him to safety, bringing together the rest of the pieces of the puzzle.

"Where do you want to go?" she asked him absently.

"Anywhere your heart desires," he lifted her chin so that she looked up into his loving look. "But first, I want to know how you got out of those ropes."

EPILOGUE

"*D*on't you come in here and tell me I can't smoke," Stella's voice was a scratchy croak, as she scowled at the nurse who'd walked through the door. "The smell of this damn hospital hurts my throat! Just go back to whatever you were doing and leave me in peace. Nobody tells me what to do."

The nurse didn't reply, didn't smile, but walked with purpose towards Stella's bed. She collected a pillow from the bed in the next bay and turned to face Stella, the pillow grasped between her hands as she loomed in the shadows.

"Do I know you? You look… familiar," Stella peered through the smoky gloom of her room, her pipe paused halfway to her mouth.

When the nurse stepped into the ring of light cast by the lamp on the bedside table, Stella reared back as recognition hit her. "Angel."

"Hello, Stella," Angela whispered.

The raspy laugh was like rocks in a metal bucket. "I was told you were dead. I saw the grave myself."

Angela reached the side of the bed, eyes dull like the edges of a rusty blade. "Dug the ruddy thing myself, told George that the plan would work – how else was I to stop you from coming after me?"

Stella relaxed against the bed as realisation hit her, accepting of her fate. "George. He always did have a soft spot for you... For all of you. I sent him after you – him, and that Billy. Turns out I underestimated that boy."

Angela laughed mirthlessly. "You underestimated my sisters, too. Look at you, broken and dying in a bed."

"That's right. After everything I did for you, look at how you all repaid me," Stella spat, the effort of her vehemence causing her chest to spasm. "Leave me in peace, Angel. I have nothing left for you. Everyone has turned on me – even my own body has forsaken me."

"I can't stop. As long as there is breath in your body, Stella, you will keep after Trixie and Lily. You, or Lizzie. It will never be over for them. I have to make it right."

The pillow was pressed down with lethal motion and Stella clawed at the air, at the arms, at the material that was pressed against her face. Eventually, she fell still. Angela calmly slid the pillow underneath the deathly still body, settled her blankets, and then she whispered a prayer of forgiveness.

She dipped her head to Stella. "It's over."

~

MONTANA TERRITORY, America.

TRIXIE STOOD on the wraparound porch of the log cabin, leaning against the railing as she looked out over the vast lake. Sunlight dappled the water, glinting like a thousand diamonds. Behind the lake, the treeline hugged rocky outcrops that soared beyond to craggy grey mountains, the snow-capped tips seemingly touching the sky. When Felix had first mentioned this as a place that they could run to, it had sounded perfect. Away from London, where no one had ever even heard of the Queen of Thieves. Seeing the area for the first time, simply took her breath away. A lazy warm breeze tousled the curls that framed her face and she hooked one behind her ear when she turned at the footfall on the boards behind her.

Felix let the cabin door slam shut behind him and he walked up behind her, wrapped his arms around her waist and she rested her forearms on his, leaning back into his embrace so that they looked across the landscape. "Have I told you that you look radiant today, Mrs Huxley?"

Trixie turned her head, rubbed the tip of her nose against her cheek. "No, husband, but the day is still young."

Felix kissed the tip of her nose, his grey eyes returning to the vista beyond them. "What do you think of my humble home?"

The cabin was indeed humble, nestled along the banks of the lake and curtained from the dirt road by Douglas fir and aspen trees. It wasn't far from a train station though and they'd been brought here by wagon. The town had been full of rustic, timber-framed buildings that had their purpose crudely listed on the exteriors in simple painted print. Townsfolk had ambled along – no sign of the frenetic energy of London or New York where cabs raced along streets at breakneck speeds.

She cast an eye over the timber frame. "I know you said that it was remote, but this is…"

"Taking it to the extreme?" Felix chuckled. "Andrew used it for hunting mostly. One of the copper mines that he bought is over in the next town. We'll go there tomorrow if you like, once you've all settled in?"

Trixie tapped a hand to the back of his. "I know that you said your uncle was wealthy, Felix, but a copper mine? What other secrets have you kept from me?"

Felix chuckled. "Well, it's nice to know that you don't know everything about me,"

"Yet," Trixie stated.

Both turned to the door when it swung wide with a squeaking protest, at Lily's objections in having been roused from her slumber. She was ushered further out onto the deck by George. He seemed to hover a moment, and paced to the railing, back to Lily.

"What is it, George? I'm so tired I could sleep on a line. What is so urgent that it can't wait until I've slept at least?" Lily grumbled, folding her arms crossly.

Trixie straightened out of Felix's embrace, watching the older man's face, taking in the way he rubbed the back of his neck and the sheepish look that he sent her way. A frisson of anxiety itched between her shoulder blades. It was because of George that they'd managed to get away – because of Maisie that Felix had escaped. "George?"

George cleared his throat, scratched at the scruff that covered his chin, and let out a long, suffering sigh. "I don't know how to tell you girls this," he began, dragging the cap off his head to smooth his cropped hair to his skull. "And I wanted to tell you, I did. I almost did a few times, over the years. Then you were away, Trix, and it was easy to put it to the back of my mind. But... I was also concerned about my own skin in the matter. It was just safer all round to keep my lip buttoned and say nothing."

Trixie exchanged a look with Felix. "Wanted to tell us what?"

"I was once sent to do a job by Stella. One that really didn't... I'm a criminal, Trixie. But I never did nothing that bad."

Frustration, exhaustion, fear made her tone sharp. "Will you just spit it out?"

"It's about Angel. There is a grave, just as Stella told you.... Only Angel wasn't ever in it." George lifted pained eyes to hers. "Angela is alive, Trix. And I know where she is."

ALSO BY ANNIE SHIELDS

Ghosts of the Mill

As Hawks Mill teeters on the brink of collapse, Lena Pemberton stands at the helm of a revolution, challenging every norm Victorian society has set.

Alone, she must navigate the treacherous waters where others believe a woman has no place at the helm. Her only hope lies with the millworkers, who urge her to seek the aid of an enigmatic engineer, Henry Wickham. He is a man of guarded emotions and a mysterious past. Lena needs his expertise to rescue the struggling mill, but Henry has encountered her kind before - profit first, safety last.

The Dockyard Darling

In the haunting aftermath of her father's sudden death, Ella Tomlinson finds herself at the mercy of her cruel stepmother, Clara. Ella uncovers Clara's dark secret and unsettling questions about her father's demise surface.

Desperate to escape a forced marriage, Ella seeks refuge with her estranged uncle in his lively tavern, hidden in the heart of London's bustling Docklands. Here, she is plunged into a dangerous world filled with sailors, boatmen, and shadowy traders.

In the Shadows of the Workhouse

In the heart of Brookford workhouse, darkness festers.

Portia Summerhill, the spirited new schoolmistress, arrives full of hope, eager to bring light into the lives of the forsaken souls trapped within its walls. Yet, as she delves deeper, a chilling truth emerges from the shadows.

Maisie Milne, a brave orphan on the brink of a new life outside the workhouse, whispers haunting tales of unspeakable deeds.

With time running out and Maisie's future hanging in the balance, Portia is drawn into a race against time, determined to unveil the harrowing secrets lurking behind closed doors. Will they unravel the truth before the clock chimes its final hour?

Step into a tale of dark mysteries and secrets lurking in the shadows of the workhouse.

ABOUT THE AUTHOR

Annie Shields lives in Shropshire with her husband and two daughters.

When she doesn't have her nose in a book, you'll find her exploring old buildings and following historical trails, dragging her ever-patient husband along with his trusty map.

If you would like to be amongst the first to hear when she releases a new book and free books by similar authors, you can join her mailing list HERE https://BookHip. com/BBMBDFM

As a thank you, you will receive a **FREE** copy of her eBook The Barefoot Workhouse Orphan - the prequel to the book In The Shadows of the Workhouse, where we meet William Finnegan and Connie for the first time.

Your details won't be passed along to anyone else and you can unsubscribe at any time.

Printed in Dunstable, United Kingdom